D0227585

ABOUT THE AUTHOR

Richard Llewellyn once called himself 'an expatriate Welshman who now lives in the world and will stay there.' When he was sixteen he went to Italy to learn hotel management, but took up painting and sculpture and learned eight languages in Venice instead. At nineteen he enlisted in the Army, and had already been a journalist, script-writer and playwright when his first novel, HOW GREEN WAS MY VALLEY, was published in 1939. By the time of his second, NONE BUT THE LONELY HEART, Llewellyn was a Captain in the Welsh Guards, serving in Italy and North Africa. Subsequently, he wrote novels set in North and South America, Italy, Africa, Israel, India and the Middle East, in all of which he had lived, but his reputation as one of the most talented and popular authors of our time is founded on the sequence of four novels: HOW GREEN WAS MY VALLEY; UP, INTO THE SINGING MOUNTAIN; DOWN WHERE THE MOON IS SMALL and GREEN, GREEN MY VALLEY NOW.

By Richard Llewellyn and published by New English Library

HOW GREEN WAS MY VALLEY
UP, INTO THE SINGING MOUNTAIN
DOWN WHERE THE MOON IS SMALL
GREEN, GREEN MY VALLEY NOW
NONE BUT THE LONELY HEART
AT SUNRISE, THE ROUGH MUSIC
TELL ME NOW, AND AGAIN
A NIGHT OF BRIGHT STARS
I STAND ON A QUIET SHORE

I STAND ON
A QUIET SHORE
Richard Llewellyn

NEW ENGLISH LIBRARY

For my brother Trevor
and
in loving memory
of our favourite uncle
Blethyn Thomas

First published in Great Britain in 1982 by Michael Joseph Ltd

Copyright © 1982 by Richard Llewellyn

All rights reserved. No part of this publication may be reproduced
or transmitted, in any form or by any means, without permission of
the publishers.

First NEL Paperback Edition August 1984

Conditions of sale: This book is sold subject
to the condition that it shall not, by way of
trade or otherwise, be lent, resold, hired out,
or otherwise circulated without the publisher's
prior consent in any form of binding or cover
other than that in which it is published and
without a similar condition including this
condition being imposed on the subsequent purchaser.

NEL Books are published by
New English Library,
Mill Road, Dunton Green,
Sevenoaks, Kent.
Editorial office: 47 Bedford Square, London WC1B 3DP

Made and printed in Great Britain by
Richard Clay (The Chaucer Press) Ltd, Bungay, Suffolk

Typeset in Times by Fleet Graphics, Enfield, Middlesex

ISBN 0 450 05717 8

I WALKED into Claridge's two minutes before a four o'clock appointment, sniffing the unchanged fragrance of privilege I ever remembered. Running into Hilsly leaving the cloakroom, I felt as if I had last seen him yesterday instead of years before. But he looked tired, pale, not a bit the man I had known. His clothes hung, and he shambled in what seemed to be loose shoes. Worse, his hands were bloated and they shook.

'This has to be short and not nearly so sweet as I'd like,' he said in a fragile voice. 'I've got to be in Zurich at nine tonight. Let's go up to my place. No disturbance.'

'How's Teheran?'

'Unbelievable. That's why we're here.'

'Whatever you want me to do's done. You know that.'

The lift went up quietly as ever.

'We're finished,' he said, staring at the grille. 'Financially and economically. My house has been burnt down. Nothing's left. The plant's destroyed. How the devil so-called technicians can smash what brings them a livelihood simply confounds me. But I don't see why it should. After all, they're not even a generation away from the desert. They learned their jobs monkey-see, monkey-do, by copying the hand-controls of our engineers. Now they're not there any more? Chaos. Unless they bring in the Russians or the Chinese. It'll be a very long time before there's the production we had. But they won't. That damned Ayatollah and the lunatics with him want another way to live. Islamic law. Sharia. Do them any good? Of course not. A mediaeval bollix!'

I followed him into the suite. A floor waiter ripped the foil off a bottle of champagne and took two frosted glasses out of the ice bucket. Hilsly dismissed him with a note and tapped the bottle.

'If you'd prefer Scotch and soda,' he said, nodding at the sideboard. 'Yes, it's been a bloody horror. Most of my friends are dead. When my chief engineer was shot I knew I'd be next. Thank God Louise isn't with us. Her collection of rugs and porcelains and all the God-knows-what, gone. Offices, files, burnt. I'm not over the shock. I never shall be. It's why oil or anything to do with it's anathema. That's why I asked you to come here instead of sending a Telex or using the radio. It's all bugged. I didn't want the details out till we'd had a talk. I'd like to issue a joint statement. Put all doubts to rest. I want to sell my share, preferably to you.'

I was simply, within the bounds of language, pole-axed. Whatever I had dreamed or fantasised, this had never been a part. To own the entire company had certainly been an ambition, but up in the clouds, beyond any hope.

It was mine.

'How much?'

He laughed, not the famous Hilsly guffaw, but a few little breaths, more like a girl starting a sobber.

'Almost old BB himself!' he said. 'Always the arch-pragmatist. Well, we were trained the same way. The figures and all the details are there. Simply look at the last page and say yes or no. I hope old BB's looking!'

I went over to the tan leather folder and turned that thick folio to the final page, and the total in red.

It was risibly small.

'I'll take it,' I said. 'That's cash?'

'On what's called the barrel-head. I want it soon and in a lump. When?'

'I'll catch the early Swissair, and I'll meet you at

6

Crédit Suisse in the Bahnhofstrasse at about ten. When we've signed, let's go to the Sprüngli for a coffee and cognac. On?'

He held out a hand.

'No trouble about liquidity?' he asked, even anxiously.

'With Crédit Suisse? Ridiculous. It'll be in your account within thirty minutes.'

'Ah, Jon!' he said. 'I'm so happy. I thought I'd have to go on the market with all that nonsense. Now it's clean and right. So much what BB would have wanted. Right down the middle. Let's have a glass together?'

'With all the pleasure in this world!'

And why not?

In that moment I was rather more than a multi-and-then-more millionaire. I was a billionaire, on a par with Saudi sheikhs and my Emir friends, but the feeling was nothing more than trying to get drunk on tea. If you have plenty of money, a little more or twice as much means very little.

What's *done* with it is what matters.

2

I WALKED back to my hotel, passing through Berkeley Square, missing so many of the old places. There was no longer that particular elegance, and I found all of it not so much shabby as drab. Most shops had become airline offices or car salesrooms. My favourite restaurant had gone. There was certainly a new hotel, but I had no wish to go in. It was not the London I once thought I knew. I had been in New York the day before and found the same malaise there. Not to improve, or add to the customer's satisfaction, but a determination to extract the last coin and to hell with any principle.

I asked the hall porter to book me on the next shuttle to Paris, with a car to take me to the airport. I had only hand luggage and a couple of cameras, and in a few minutes I was off. But those minutes were important in a way I had never thought about before.

'The possession of money in itself carries responsibility,' BB—Beaulieu Blount—had once said to me. 'The more money, the more responsibility for making it work. It is our economical lifeblood. The more it is used, the healthier the economy. Thrift is a poor man's prerogative. Wealth used shrewdly and always with an eye to the future brings healthy profit, the oil in the machine. Without it, nothing works because nothing is worth working *for*. Working men and women have made that plain through the efforts of their unions, though unfortunately the best brains are not among their leaders. Most of them are merest clerks without a decent idea. Only the power of their voting hordes sustains them or gives them the right to speak. A worthless lot.'

I had forgotten neither the words nor the tone of voice, or his habit of tearing up his notes in timed, deliberate rips. It had never occurred to me to take them out of the waste-basket and paste them together. I wish it had. He had been in the Um'm Sham'ms area for more than fifty years, and he knew everybody and everybody's child, and he was loved whether for himself or what he could do, and he was able to do plenty. By his intervention, all the boys and girls of Emirate families went to school in England or Switzerland or in the United States, and as a result their people had enormous benefit. Modern housing began to be built, water was piped, electricity shone in the streets and in their homes. Soon their children had excellent schools, and hospitals saved many from the graveyard, which in that place was a space of ground where not even a mound or a pile of stones gave hint of burial. I liked that. When the vital dust settled against the stones and blessed the dry earth, there was nothing more to be said or done. Get on with it. That was the Arab way, and I agreed.

I went there as an orphan, little more than fifteen, glad to leave the regimentation of school and post-war rationing behind. I was sent out by BB to be an office boy, to be the legs of Mr Fruark. By that time he needed them, though his mind was clear as a gem, and he usually spoke with the precision of an actuary. I was young, yes, but capable and easily trained. Once all the tanker captains knew me I never had a moment's trouble, and the days skimmed along between paperwork, falconing and fishing. In those days there weren't many of us, and five Arab clerks translated English into Arabic for the Emir over the water. His major-domo came across every night except on Friday, the Muslim day of rest, and Sunday, ours.

That was how I met Khalil, the Emir's eldest son, on holiday from Eton, and began a years-long friendship.

He was tall as me, thin, handsome in the Arab way, and he always dressed in Arab style. After a few weeks, I bought excellent clothes from his tailor over in the Emirate and found them far more comfortable to wear in the heat than trousers and a shirt. In the office, of course, I wore only the linen business suit and a collar and tie because Frukey—we called him that behind his back—would not permit anything else. Now I know the extent of discipline among men of his status, of his time. They were of a different breed, upright in all their dealings and honourable in all their ways. They were devoted to a particular way of being, a daily religion, and any slightest departure became a crime, without any excuse.

9

That is true.

I know it now, in an age of pot-bellied pygmies ready to barter their souls for extra money, in plain English, a bribe. I have had the acute displeasure of meeting so many of them, often of having to pay them, because not to would have done us damage. I wish I could pinpoint when this practice began and when it became common. It was not in the early days. I think it began in New York and spread to London and to Paris. It was like an influenza, infecting us and stretching all the way over to Baghdad, Damascus, Teheran and Riyadh. There were a lot of people to pay off, and the more oil we contracted for, the more money we needed. Without that money we could whistle for business. I knew little about that side because all our traffic was controlled from London, and BB was not the man to confide in anyone, far less pay a bribe, yet business dictated that he had to conform, and to keep tankers going, he paid.

In those days I was innocent, and oil manifests with the big purple stamp on them meant no more than the other print. But that stamp made known the amount paid on the shipment. To the crooks.

I am quite unsure how long we remain innocent, those of us, that is, outside the world—and we were well outside it, or at least I was. All I had in my little world were the details of the job, those hours, and my small oiled boat for fishing. It supplied us with the best fish, and Ibn, the major-domo, sold the rest to Zazi and split the take with me.

Zazi—that wasn't her real name—ran the bar down at the wharf. She had been a nurse put ashore from a tanker. Frukey brought a doctor from Bahrein and he said she had yellow fever, and she stayed with us for about a month, nursed by two nuns from the college up the road. It was not yellow fever but a kind of malaria, and BB sent out medicines, and she moved down the road to the wharfage and built up a bar and eating place for the tanker sailors. With girls.

'What's the hell's use of a bar in a place like this without girls?' she said to me, that time. 'These men are hungry. They want fresh food and good drinks and women. So? I supply.'

But not with Bedouin or Arab women. The Emir would have had the place burnt down. She got them from Beirut and other places, most Somali and Ethiopian, parts of the world where people starved and women paid for food with their bodies. For a couple of months after the opening, I was not allowed in there, which made me all the more determined to go in and see what went on. My chance came when Ibn went on harvest leave, and I took a morning's catch down there and tied up at the wharf.

Zazi's place was built on a pebbly beach well back from the tide. A long, low, two-storey barn with air-conditioners instead of windows, it was whitewashed and its red front door glinted large brass handles.

Zazi saw me when I went in and came hurrying from behind the bar. She wore a white overall of some thin stuff and a beaded belt and cap, with long gold earrings. Girls sat at every table with about a dozen men in all, and all of them drunk as—sailors.

'You know perfectly well you're not allowed in here!' Zazi said, and pointed. 'Go round the back. I'll meet you there. Mister Fruark'd have a fit!'

I went out and around to the kitchen door. The place was clean as a surgery, and a couple of maids were chopping potatoes in chips, and a big woman in starched whites came from a smaller room behind the stove to take my basket and lift it on the scales.

'I've told you twenty times to put the *fish* on the scales, not the *basket*!' Zazi screeched behind me. 'Every time I turn m' back I'm getting done. Now weigh

11

the fish and be sharp about it. Helpless bloomin' lot!'

The cook glanced at her, started weighing the fishes, and spoke to the scale dial.

' 'At basket, she weighin' two pounds, and all I do's takin' two pounds off the total,' she said, all in the same tone. 'I don't want you comin' in my kitchen and talkin' rude in front of everybody. I'm from the mission school an' I don' like swear words. Any more an' I *go*. I *mean* it!'

'Now, now, duckie, don't take on!' Zazi said, and laid a hand on her shoulder. 'I won't lose you for the sake of bad temper. You're the best cook I've ever had. I owe for fourteen-and-a-half pounds, is that it?'

'That's it. The little 'uns, they'll go in the soup. I wish he bring me more the big 'uns. They cut big steaks.'

'Groupers are hard to find,' I said. 'I need stronger tackle and some lures.'

'Give me a list and I'll ask one of the captains to buy it,' Zazi said. 'One's going up to Alexandria tonight. He'll be back next week. Give me a list. Cost you nothing.'

But next morning Mr Fruark had me in the office. News travels fast.

'You were told not to go near Zazi's place,' he said, looking at me over his glasses. 'You were there yesterday. I know you went to sell her your catch. But you dis-obeyed an order. Why?'

'Sir, there was nobody else to—'

'Rubbish! There was Fuad and a couple of others. In future you will be careful *not* to go there. I don't want to have to write to Mister Blount that you've caught syphilis or *what*ever. What do you think *he'd* do? Chuck you out. Thought of that? Don't do it again. Or get ready to pack!'

'Very well, sir. I'm sorry.'

'And another thing. What's this about sea captains

being asked to do your shopping for you? Captains of ships are not at your pleasure. Take those ideas out of your head. Do you suppose they like the idea that some half-baked office boy can tell them to do this, that, and the other? Don't *dare* do it again. Understood?'

I was filled with a sense of injustice that seemed to burn, but there was nothing to say. I had gone there in defiance of an explicit order, and the rest was makeweight, unimportant. But it taught me a lesson.

Any thought of leaving Um'm Sham'ms really did horrify me. I had nowhere to go. I knew nobody. I spoke English and Arabic with equal ease. But beyond the people I worked with I had no friends except Khalil. I was very much self-centred, and perfectly happy. But when I looked at that dot on the globe Mr Fruark had on his desk, and realized that I was a dot inside it, I had some notion of how important I was. A little nothing. Words could never have said it for me. I had to see it. A dot inside a dot, and nothing more. Mr Fruark was a dot, and so was Mrs Pincus, the accountant. Dots. So was everybody, everywhere. Simply little dots. And they all went into the ground, among the sand and rocks.

I believe I grew up at that moment, though I am far from sure how. I only knew that I was a dot, and in some peculiar way I felt older.

But I lost all that when Khalil came over in the launch with his rods bought in London and New York, and a box of lures on four platforms that simply did dazzle. And yet, even with my old line and the hooks baited with fat sardines and strips of raw mutton, I caught three times as many fish, and just at the end, a grouper longer than the stretch of my arms, its enormous head filled with teeth I knew Zazi's cook would love. She made necklaces of them. Khalil was jealous, and his looks at the grouper told me that he would give an arm to catch one. He never wanted to be second in anything, and I

13

understood that feeling. I baited my line again and gave it to him, and he sat on the gunwale and dropped it in, while I used his heavy rod with a red lure I had wanted since I had first seen it.

I caught another grouper, bigger and even fatter than the first. Khalil was white with fury and his lips twitched. Princely temper is not to be ignored, and when I cut out the hook I tapped the fish with the rod.

'That's yours,' I said, and no sooner than his line jerked taut and he almost went overboard. I grabbed him by the waist, and together we played that fish here and there, but a grouper rarely fights and we hauled it aboard in minutes, the biggest hunk of fish I ever saw.

'*That's* yours,' I said. 'But hang on to the teeth for Zazi's cook. She makes beautiful necklaces.'

'What do you know of Zazi?' he asked, taking a Leica out of the bag. 'Please, take my picture. I'll sit on its head. It's a big brute, isn't it?'

'The biggest. We must be running over a shoal. That's unusual.'

'I simply want to show it to my father. Then you may sell it, teeth and all. Zazi?'

'She threw me out. Mister Fruark's orders. I'm not allowed in there.'

He lifted his head to laugh, and I saw the pink of his throat.

'Really, the Calvinists are the end!' he said. 'We have that sort of puritan, too. An utter nuisance. These idiots want to bring in Islamic law. But it's long out of date. It's infantile. In countries selling millions of barrels of oil? Monstrous. They should do what we and a few more did. Bring in houses, water, electricity, and give everybody a weekly payment. Their share of the millions. Simple? But it works. The majority are not greedy. Give them what they think is a fair share, everybody getting the same and where they don't have to work for it, where they can switch on a light and turn a tap for water, and what more do they want? Cinema, radio, television? It's there. My father is extremely forward-looking. We have an excellently well-trained army. And this, unfortunately, is possibly the last time I can come and fish with you. That's why I'm really delighted with this catch. I have to do my military training. For that reason, take the rods and the lure box. They're yours, and so is the launch. I'll send it over tomorrow and it will bring you to visit me. Then you will see what Zazi has *not* got. *Really* beautiful women. Her place is a disease-ridden joke. Visit me tomorrow!'

Well.

This was princely gift-making.

But when I told Mr Fruark, he put his hands to his head, looking up.

'I've been fearing this,' he said, walking to the window and turning. 'Fearing it. Now, listen to me and learn. You'll have to go there, that's plain as a pike-staff. You can't pretend not to have had an invitation. It has to be obeyed. But be well and properly advised and warned. When you get in among them, never let your eyes rest on any one of them. You'll be watched from every window, crack and crevice. Never lay a hand on any of them. They'll tempt you, be certain of it. Everything a woman can find to do to egg a man on, they'll *do*. Be sure of *that*. What *you* have to do is take things in stride. You want *none* of them. Don't in any way *touch* them. Remember those watching eyes. Go through them at a rough pace and go *out*. Am I making myself clear?'

'Sir,' I said. 'But why am I invited there?'

'To test you. Arabians will take any woman of ours, anywhere, and pay her. But they do not permit their women to become playthings of others. Understand? You *do* understand, don't you?'

'I think I do.'

'I hope to God you do. Remember, if you set a hand on any of them and go into the cushions, you're finished. You'll never do any business here. You'll find all ways cut. You won't fill a tanker, far less a storage bunker. Anything you want, so easy before, will be *no*. Papers, passes, goodbye. You laid a hand where you shouldn't have, and that's enough. Have I convinced you?'

'Sir,' I said. 'But supposing they lay hands on me?'

'Push them aside. Have absolutely no dealings with them. They belong to one man. His is the harem. You're an outsider on test. Stay an outsider. Never consider yourself any kind of privileged guest. You are *not*. You are simply a busy bee in a hive of honey. Be careful. You can make a disastrous mistake!'

I took that thought away with me. It's been with me ever since. Never fool with Arabian women. Beautiful as they may be, they can be poison because their men are adamantine and so is their law, and the Arabs are a fierce people. They have no room for compassion and mercy is unknown.

That afternoon I had a great deal to think about.

3

I TOOK the shuttle to Paris to catch the flight to Zurich and signed into the Baur au Lac, where BB had long ago made a suite into a company residence. I went in with a feeling of coming home, for my Telex had warned of arrival, and huge bowls of roses sent a wonderful aroma everywhere, against a backdrop, as it were, of all the thousands of cigars smoked in that apartment over the years.

The business at Crédit Suisse was finished within the hour, and I signed a draft, and Hilsly and I left our files with the lawyers and bankers, and went across the road to the Sprüngli for that coffee and cognac. We found it good as ever, and the waitresses as charming. Nothing had changed in Switzerland. In fact, most things always seemed to get better, and of course, by our standards, fallen so catastrophically in past years, their government provides an excellent example of how to control and direct an economy.

'What do you intend to do?' I asked Hilsly.

'Put a little in banks to earn money, and build a factory for the microchip business. After I've had a thorough look at it. I think it and its allied industries are the business of the future. We have to think of the approaching war, haven't we?'

'Have we?'

'What's to happen when the Shah dies? Everybody knows he's got cancer. Who's going to rule? What happens to the oil we need?'

'I'm no strategist. So long as I can keep Um'm Sham'ms going, I'll be perfectly happy.'

He shook his head doomfully.

'Won't be long,' he said. 'They have a hold on our currency. We were stupid to let them. But bankers are greedy. They only see profits. Politicians are dense. They practise outdated theory. It doesn't fit the facts, and the facts are that billions of our cash goes into Arabian accounts and will continue going in for the foreseeable future. Unless the monetary system is changed. Throughout the world. While petrodollars pour in I don't see it happening. I'm getting into something new and clean. Oil's a dirty business. You'll soon find out.'

I had already found out, but I said nothing.

We were in a bad way, but there was nothing we could do. We had no army or navy or air force except in the

Emirate. Iran lay to our north-east, and Pakistan to the south beyond, with a magnificent mountain range between, thank God, which made us almost impregnable. No Iranian army could cross the only possible pass, which a well-armed brigade could defend. We were safe from attack, except by sea, parachute drop—highly unlikely—or bombing from the air.

That was my problem, and tough to solve. The forces of the Emir lay across the water. If we were attacked, he must hesitate. To land his troops to fight an invader would invite an attack on his own territory. He was impotent to do anything. So were we. One of his British officers had told me our chances of survival ran from slim to nil.

Recruiting a mercenary force seemed ridiculous. Where were they to be barracked? And how supplied? We were stocked almost daily by our incoming tankers and local Bedouin gardeners, but they could never supply rations for a couple of thousand men—even so few—and forage for their horses.

Our place had been there for more than fifty years, a half-way stop between Karachi and Alexandria to take on fresh water and greenstuff from the markets of Khorram-shahr, just up the coast.

When I first got there the place had been a square building of mud brick inside a twenty-foot wall, with the office on the ground floor and living quarters upstairs, though Mr Fruark had his own rooms behind his office below. It was an austere existence, but as a boy I had never been used to luxury, and riding in the early morning and fishing in the afternoon made up a full day, especially when Khalil came over with his falcons and we galloped into the desert to hunt anything that moved.

'Are you really going to hang on?' Hilsly asked, over the second cognac. 'Risky, isn't it?'

'I suppose it is. But I'm obstinate. When my friends

round about tell me that things are getting umpty, I'll think again.'

'Friends?'

'The Bedouin. They know everything from bazaar gossip. There isn't a move they don't know about. When they tell me trouble's on the way, I'll think of shifting.'

'But if the PLO can get a few batteries of guns across the neck up the coast and start knocking out the tankers, what then?'

'We'll need a few warships!'

'From?'

'Us. Western Europe generally. The United States?'

'They don't want another Vietnam.'

'That's dry stuff. There was no well there. Without *this* oil none of us can live. Worth fighting for?'

'Probably. But I doubt the governments will take on the job. The people won't want it.'

'So industry comes to a halt?'

'Better than war. Casualties.'

'Can't you think any other way? The Russians are going in there to take over the oilfields. Then what?'

'I don't think fighting the Russians'll do any good.'

'They're as far off their base as we are. And they've got China over their shoulder and behind their back. I think they've got a hell of a lot more to worry about than we have.'

'We?'

'The United States—the West.'

He finished his cognac in a head-back gulp.

'I'm so damn glad I'm out of it,' he said. 'If you want me I'll be at my estate in Scotland or in Hawaii. Most beautiful places in the world. They'll do me till I'm ready for the worms. That part of the world can go to hell. I spent my best years trying to make it better. But they didn't treat the ordinary people right. Very few got a fair shake. They should have done what the Kuwaitis and

Qataris and the Emir across the way did. Build them good housing, pipe in the water, and install electric light. Pay them a weekly handout. That way, the common people support you. But the Shah spent it on hardware instead of humans. Instead of making friends he imprisoned. Every time he imprisoned he made enemies. It's not the way to build a country. It'll be paid for. Mullahs are not part of this century. That'll be learned. After grief and suffering. By ordinary people. They're not getting any more now than under Mossadegh. How long will it last this time? *Not* long!'

He puffed out his cheeks and stared tiredly into a corner. He simply did not look like the architect of a new industry—one, incidentally, I had hardly heard of, except for items in the newspapers, without having much notion of what they meant.

'What exactly is this microchip business?' I asked him.

He got up, stretching.

'I'm too exhausted to start going into it,' he said. 'You'll have to forgive me. I'll ask the London office to send you some coggage. You'll know as much as I do. I haven't really looked at it. But it's an investment. You could do worse than take a fat batch of shares. In what I believe's the future. They'll never know what hit them!'

'Who?'

'Us. And the rest of the world.'

'Why?'

'Different way of thinking. Of living. Of working. Dynamic. Explosive and destructive. It'll expose us to the age of leisure. There's magic and disaster in that. It presupposes boredom. Odd that a quondam aristo-sickness should inflict itself on the poverty-stricken. I'm not a bit confident of the future. The majority aren't educated. They know little more than trade-unionism. So swinishly ignorant that it sets the teeth on edge. We're in a bad way. Thank *God* I'm out of it!'

'Doesn't sound too promising?'

'The reverse. I think we're in for a very hard time. The work force led by idiots against the elected Government. It won't wash. I can't guess what's going to happen but doubtless there'll be a few bodies. A bloodlet will prevent what's happening in Iran. Utter chaos. And we don't know a fraction of it. God help us all!'

'You believe in God?'

'As I believe I had a mother and father. They're not alive and I can't prove it, but that's my belief. I'm off for a snooze. What're you doing?'

'Going back to Paris to take Concorde to Bahrein. I'll be there tonight in time for dinner. Looking back only a few years, what a miracle that is!'

He nodded.

'But the poor old girl looks like being shoved into limbo for the sake of the economy,' he said. 'What a bloody stupid way of doing things, isn't it? Spend millions, achieve the forefront of air technology, and for the sake of mere money, nothing more than figures on a balance sheet, you scrap it. I don't know. I give up. To hell with it!'

That low tone of despair I seemed to feel in our parting handshake—thought raising defeatism to a massive level—was beyond me, and anyway he had almost twenty years' more experience and I had no wish to argue. But it reminded me of something Frukey once said.

'Don't get too comfortable here,' he said, looking about. 'It's a lovely place, but don't get any funny ideas. We haven't got much time. They've seen what an easy job we've made of it. They'll want to do it on their own. They'll give us the shove. All of us. Then they'll take over. Easy?'

'Doesn't seem fair.'

''Course it's fair. It's their stuff. Their land. We had

21

the idea we could run industries off their blood. After all, oil *is* the blood of Arabia. We were making fortunes out of it. Now they make fortunes out of us. Fair? I think so. I've always found the Arabs a splendid people. Very honest. If *you* are. If you're not, they'll teach you a lesson. Don't give them the opportunity. See it my way?'

'Yes.'

'Good.'

4

KHALIL CAME over that pale-blue stretch, in his dhow-cum-yacht that ballooned an arc of pinkish lateen sail, a lovely picture. He used the wheel as a veteran to come alongside so that I could step aboard without a pause, and he turned the boat in almost its own length to dip its prow into shining water again.

Khalil had sailed from infancy, and Huq—his close-clipped greybeard helmsman—had been his mentor. It was generally known that, at eighteen, Khalil was among the best watermen in those parts. That was the reason I wondered at his ignorance of fishing, but I had not known that fishing was not taught. Fishing was for fishermen and the catch earned a living. Princes did not need to earn a living. The sporting instinct was confined to dogs, hawks, and falcons, though Khalil liked nothing better than catching a fish the size of a grouper, and so I put out lines. But I think we always travelled too fast in his yacht, and we never caught anything worth hanging up from the mast to show everybody. Khalil was always a little miffed, as if his magnificent boat had some sort of curse upon it, though my small one of oiled timbers and a patched orange sail brought them up one after another. I tried to explain to him that speed was a factor. If you go through the water too fast, your line is drawn up and the hooks trail behind only to catch the smaller fish. The grouper finds its food deeper down, and you have to go slower to hang the bait where you can entice a bite. Khalil never quite got the idea until that afternoon. Then, in a real blaze of temper, he turned the yacht and insisted we go back and man my boat—a poor idiot beside his—and Huq glanced at me sideways and shut his eyes tight in a smile so that I knew he agreed. In the next hour we caught four groupers, and if we had not been in such a hurry we might have caught many more, but we had to get his yacht over to the other side, where his father was waiting.

'This is the last time I can come out,' Khalil said. 'Tomorrow I fly to London. I join the Royal Military Academy. I'll come back as an officer in my father's army. I'll no longer need this yacht. I shan't have the time. It's yours. With your pilot, Huq!'

Well. More princely gifts.

What do you say?

You bend your head, and you say nothing.

Princes do not require to be thanked.

That is the royal Arab way.

I went ashore behind Khalil and into the palace, a new building of many windows on the shade side, none on the others, but blotched by air-conditioners all in a roar, and dripping.

Guards stood at three doors on the shade side, tall men with drawn scimitars, and they divided smartly for us to pass into a cool foyer, and automatic doors opened into a huge room of plants and flowers and a floor covered with carpets and heaps of cushions, a couple of thrones with gold insignia on the high backs, and the biggest divan I ever saw. Fifty or more women stood in silence,

23

all veiled, with nothing, not even hands, showing. I saw nothing to tempt me.

Khalil sat in the smaller of the two thrones, and a footman put an armchair behind me.

Khalil turned, smiling.

'Take which of them you like,' he said, nodding at the women. 'Choose one or two or three if you wish. That's what they're here for.'

'But I'm not,' I said.

'Then what *are* you here for?'

'To be presented, I thought, to His Excellency the Emir?'

'You have all the answers,' he said, and got up. 'Very well. Let's go to the library. I'm sorry you don't like our women!'

'I didn't *say* that. It's simply that Arabian women are for Arabian men. They are not gifts for foreigners!'

'You *have* all the answers!' he said. 'I'm glad. I could send a nice little non-Arabian across to you? As a pet, if you like?'

'It would cause gossip. There is the office staff over there. They wouldn't like it. My pets are confined to cats and dogs. They are my constant companions. Would you care for a Siamese queen?'

'I'd care for nothing better if I were staying here. But what is a Siamese?'

'A cat of a very particular order. She or he will talk to you!'

'Nonsense!'

'Let me send you one and find out!'

'Send one to the princess I shall marry. He or she will speak for me!'

'On. The address?'

He wrote and I took the paper.

'I thought of getting an Alsatian to protect her.'

'Leave it to me. The Doggo Argentino's a new breed,

24

especially trained to hunt the Argentinian boar. You could call him a boar hound. He has no fear. In any event, he hasn't any appetite for sheep or goats!'

'I've heard about them. Why haven't I got one?'

'You never made the effort. It would've been easy enough. When you get back, I'll have a Doggo, two bitches and—depending on the season—a litter of pups. They'll do your heart good, and you'll know she'll be safe. On that, you may bet a real wad!'

'I'm delighted. Please!'

Two swordsmen opened double doors, and Khalil gestured.

We went into a room almost exactly a copy of the Um'm Sham'ms main office, though twice its size and with many more books. The Emir, in a shantung silk suit, came around the desk holding out his hand in welcome, and looked at Khalil.

'How dare you come here dressed in that manner?' he said, quietly. 'Get off and change. Immediately!'

Without turning, I heard Khalil make an obeisance and walk smartly to the door, and out.

'These young fellows are spoiled by the women,' he said. 'They need a touch of the whip. They become careless, and suddenly everything is careless. That's why I so greatly admire the way your business is controlled on the other side. I need hardly tell you that I keep close watch. On you and the others. I find no weakness. But you are excellently well trained. For such a young man you act in a most extraordinarily capable manner. It is my hope and my prayer that my son will comport himself in the same way!'

'I'm sure he will.'

'I know I'm under sentence of death at all times. Any gunman can earn a great fortune by killing me. It will *not* prevent my going about my country and talking to people and showing them that I have no fear. If anything

25

happens to me, I hope that you and Khalil will liaise. On the oil front you can be of great help to him. On this side, of course, you cannot do much. He will have his army advisors. They admit very little civil interference. Look. I want your tanker captains to be given specific instructions to examine the coast on both sides from the time they leave your wharfage until they pass the neck, that is, Alexandria-bound. A few batteries of guns on both sides could wreck our entire fleet. You appreciate that?'

'It has been appreciated for many months.'

'And?'

'We have no arms, sir. We have ships to take oil from here to there. We prosecute peaceful trade. Why should we think of guns?'

'Because others think of them!'

He got up, lighting his pipe—a Dunhill straightgrain with a gold crown on the rim, tipped with turquoise and amethyst droplets—and puffed an aroma of Sobranie.

'I don't think the world appreciates the daily threat we have to contend with,' he said, quietly. 'We have an army facing us in the hills over there. They are supplied by a variety of bastards. They'd like to take this entire territory. The Emirates. They would have access to a supply of oil. They would achieve a strangle-hold on the Western markets. All they'd need is a few gun teams on both sides of the neck. Sink a few tankers. That brings in the navies of Europe and America. It might bring in the Soviets. It would possibly mean the end of *us*. But I want to leave this territory to my son. Is that unreasonable?'

'I shall help all I may.'

'Good. Then small-toothcomb the soukh on your side. Give me the names and go into the backgrounds of every man in trade. Any new arrival without means, *or* trade. They're all suspect. I can't send my own people over. They'd be spotted. The clans here are all instantly recognizable, and that's a disadvantage. You will do that for me?'

'Immediately I get back, sir.'

'I'm so glad Khalil has someone his own age as a friend he can rely on. I'm sending a platoon of guards to strengthen you. Can't take any risks these days. They'll supply their own rations and forage. No trouble.'

'You expect trouble, then?'

He nodded.

'From any side,' he said. 'At any time. Primarily from the sea. It's a coast of pirates. I shall send an officer tomorrow and he'll advise on defence. Meanwhile, Khalil is my only worry. He goes tomorrow, thank God, and we have two years to breathe easily. Every time he went with his falcons to the desert with you, I tasted my heart in my throat. But he is a man. Should I keep him behind curtains as a woman? Impossible. He is my son. A *soldier*!'

He held out his hand.

'We shall speak again,' he said, with a smile. 'In a couple of months we might fly to London and see him at the Academy. Would you like that?'

'Sir, very much. But I'd have to get permission.'

He waved his hand.

'Simply say that I invite, and I request. It should be all!'

5

THAT TALK stuck in my mind, too. It was a first warning, although at the time I never gave it a thought in those terms. I know now that he saw what was coming. I was really not much more—as Frukey had once said—than a jumped-up office boy, capable in a small area, able to manipulate within certain entirely industrial bounds, but quite incapable of thinking beyond, far less to the future. For me, it meant tankers coming in to discharge, and taking on freights and going elsewhere. There seemed nothing further to be done. In that area I was more than competent, and the tanker captains made me chairman at their annual dinners to present a prize to the captain with the most mileage and tonnage for the year.

Between pipe-puffs I heard the quiver in the Emir's voice—a voice made hoarse by parade-ground commands to more than two thousand men, and that takes throat muscles and lungs. Yet on that day he seemed to whisper. The whisper is still with me. He seemed to be a father talking over my shoulder, but I was too dull to hear what he said.

Dull.

In that day we were all dull.

But I had my job to do, and it seemed the be-all and the end-all. There was shock in finding that it certainly left an area of doubt, whether in the paper on my desk or in the wall-graphs where a story was told for all to see.

Andy Giorgiakis, one of our best captains, gave me a first hint. He always carried a silver cane with an onyx-and-ivory head, and he pointed it at the far graph, and said that a lot more oil seemed to be going to Rotterdam —though none of our tankers were used to take it there—only to be redirected to other ports with the cargo sold and another to take on, which often meant cleaning out the tanks, a short voyage to do it, and a higher cost to the buyer. Or else they went direct to Rotterdam, and on to another port with new papers and a higher price, nearly always to the United States or sometimes to Japan or to Germany. The entire business confused me, and I called Frukey in Bahrein.

'Look,' he said, in what sounded like a spray of steam from a winch—our radio interference—'we're in the oil business. Hear what I said? *Business.* It's where you sell for the most you can get and buy for the least. BB saw this coming years ago. I've lived to see it. Just get it into your head. It's a business. They all want oil. They'll pay the price. We're in the middle. Got that? Well, sleep on it and don't lose any. We've got the tankers, and we can put up our prices, too. All's fair in love and war. This, Jon, is war. Make up your mind to it. Everything else all right? Fine. I'll be back the week after next, Friday. Take care, won't you?'

I was left wondering, even, perhaps, with a little fear, though I could never have given any reason for it. Instinct, sharpened by experience, it may have been. But it left a thoroughly uncomfortable feeling as of walking in a black night along an unknown tunnel. I have no idea when that extraordinary ability lodged and became a part of my conscious self, but it did, and I have to be grateful, because I could always see a problem coming and evade it or meet it head-on.

We had so many problems even then. Ships' crews out of love with their officers stayed ashore, dug holes in the desert around Zazi's and put a couple of goatskins under, and a couple over, and slept with the gods, and when they were ready there was always a tanker to take them on, on and on. And either they slept rough and spent the last penny on booze, or they became men to be trusted, and we always took great care of them.

Mrs Pincus had their files, thousands of them, and she could always supply a crew on the instant that even the most pernickety captain could not fault. From Lascars down all the nationalities to our own, every one of them was first-class. It was at that time I was brought to see the optimum in human nature.

The best were the best, and the worst were worthless.

29

It always held. Hamid, my houseman, I had found in the desert during an early morning gallop. I had half-seen that raised arm and heard the call, and we picked him up and took him down to the nuns, and a couple of weeks later he limped into my office and held out his hands, and I liked his eyes. From that moment he took charge of my office and rooms, and they sparkled. How that happens between a life in a tent and four walls filled with furniture is something I have never understood, but it did. He seemed to know exactly what to do. I never had to teach him anything. But there was an extraordinary plus. His brothers and uncles and cousins and the men of his clan came in day after day to be grooms and falconers, and fishermen, and house-guards, and we soon had a large staff, all of them refusing pay, even food. But then I found out that the Emir was supplying them.

I had a considerable moral debt to the Emir. There was nothing I could do to pay him. The suggestion was in itself ridiculous and I would never have mentioned it, though I made sure every detail of our business was reported immediately to his desk.

Thus the report from the captain of the *Peerless Royal* that building was going on south of the neck in mountainous country led to Hamid's clan, with the Emir's support, riding out there and blowing up and burying everybody, something that never appeared in print. But what could happen once could happen again. We began to mount desert patrols. This had nothing to do with me or the company. But it did. We would have been stupid to ignore the threat, and so began the early morning patrols that soon became routine. They also became a rich source of profit, because the enemy were killed to a man, and their horses and camels, arms and property, were sold in the soukh once the clansmen had taken what they wanted. A Kalashnikov rifle commands a high price, even higher with ten clips of bullets. Those details had no interest for me. I wanted to know where those troops and builders had come from, but because there were no survivors there was nobody to question. The rest was a guess. I believe the Emir knew, but he never said a word and I thought it wiser to leave it.

Until the morning Hamid in his scarlet robe came into the office like a swirling sandstorm and said a large column of troops was riding towards us, and we should get the women out immediately to the Emirate.

I called Frukey, and he said, 'Right. Leave it to me, but stand by. Get the girls packed and ready. Take plenty of food. Don't forget water. Out.'

In about an hour the Emirate's coastline, what little we could see, appeared to froth in the wakes of marine landing craft, and fighters screamed over us and out to the desert, and then we heard the bombs. The girls were there, and Hamid, Fuad, and Ibn stood ready as Abd rode past with his clansmen, a surprising number, more than two hundred before I lost count. I could see nothing through my binoculars except clouds of dust far to the left, but then the landing craft were sliding up the beach and the Emir's troops jumped ashore and passed by us going into the desert, piled on half-tracks, tanks, and armoured cars.

The troop commander shouted over engine tumult that the small helicopter would come back for me, and a plane was ready to take us all to Bahrein. I told him I intended asking the pilot to take me over the battle-ground to find out what was happening, and he shrugged and shut the door. Wise man. Had I had the smallest concept of what modern battle meant, I would have let it go on without me.

It took only that short bumpy flight in the down-draught of fighters to reach the end of our column, the van of the attackers, bodies piled in heaps, arms, legs, and glaring heads, and I shouted to the pilot to turn

31

back, and we swung up and away for the sea and—thankfully enough—for the airstrip. A few miles, a few minutes, for the sanity of silence and a world at peace, but I had time to wonder how a few men in their idiocy could send hundreds of the anonymous to death or grievous wounds without hope of succour. I had looked for a Red Crescent unit but there was none. We had ambulances behind the half-tracks, though with no sign of their being used. Then I remembered the bombers, and they were passing us in screaming low dives, a whisk that tipped us, and gone. Down on the flat land, so pleasing to the feet and mind, an aircraft waited for me, with faithful Hamid sitting on a heap of luggage.

A roaring shadow came over, the Emir jumped down from the helicopter, and I walked to meet him.

'They seek destruction and they meet it,' he said. 'Who denies it? It is wrong. So utterly wrong. Why should one Muslim community war on another? Why should there be deaths? Who gives the orders? Who pretends to command? You have only to look at the Koran to know this is wrong!'

'I had the same thought,' I said. 'A few miles away there are bodies and limbs, and the vultures are flying. The human eye is a tidbit!'

'A horrible notion. It's strange. Before this oil business came along we had a quite different life. More peaceful. Not so modern. I am almost sure that "modern" for us has no advantage. We can build houses, schools, hospitals. We can put in sewage and electricity and pay weekly sums to everyone. Do we enjoy life as much? No. Nobody works. Nobody *has* to. Our workmen are from the outside. You're going to find your position here increasingly risky. I'd prefer you left altogether. I don't want to be held responsible for your lives, but you're certainly in danger. They can attack at any time. You know that?'

32

'But who?'

'A nice mixture of Yemenis, Libyans, and the rest. They're well paid. What do you think you will do?'

'Wait for orders from London.'

He laughed, putting a hand on my shoulder.

'You're all the same,' he said. 'Let me know when you have a reply. Meantime, I'll have another cavalry squadron here, and two more helicopters. That should take care of any emergency.'

'Sir.'

'A space of desert, sea, and sky was all around me, but a far deeper distance was in my mind. Where could I go from the life I loved? Where, from the land I had grown to think of as my own? I began to feel some of the anguish that plagued so many in the last days of the Empire, in India. Where to go? What to do?'

Like them, I had no answer, or any idea, or the smallest notion.

I only knew I had an ache in the throat, and a desire to cry as an infant. My toys were being taken from me.

I had no defence.

The Emir's flight whispered down to silence in locust-whirr, and the wind was heard again. I could feel in pain the wheeze of grief in my lungs.

6

CHRISTMAS AT Um'm Sham'ms had been the same since the time I was sent there. We all took a half-day off on December the fifteenth to put up decorations of paper chains, big paper bells, holly and mistletoe sent out from London, the big Christmas tree brought in on a tanker, and all the other stuff from years before, including the sleigh and the papier-mâché reindeer, and the Santa Claus suit always worn by Frukey. The staff loved it. The Bedouin brought their own gifts of brightly coloured rugs and wall blankets, woven through the year, so that when the dining room, common room, and main foyer were finished, the effect was startling, one delight after another.

'When I was first here, they thought I was puggled,' Frukey told me. 'But years went by and they came to expect it, especially the turkey and Christmas pudding. Oh, the *fuss* they made, and the way they chipped in? They'd never take a penny piece for anything they brought, and one time there, I thought I'd forbid their gifts. But the *uproar*!'

In the long office, where all the secretaries worked, the decoration was left to them, and they did a marvellous job, with a smaller tree down at the end that the two Japanese girls, Nobu Watanabe and Toshi Ohida, dressed in their own way, a joy of light and colour, and when Brudenal—the port electrician—and his team put up all the little electric lights among the hanging chains and the pine branches, and said they were ready to switch on, Frukey called all the Bedouin around him and held up the watch face, waiting for six o'clock, and everybody fell silent, straining for miracles. He snapped the case shut and nodded to Brudenal, down the corridor, to push the switch, and long strings of light shone and sparkled, a small glory, and the Bedu with one voice shouted 'Allahu Akhbar!' and many of the older men wept streaming tears and went to kiss Frukey's hand.

They called him, in Arabic, the Right Hand. Not—because that would have been blasphemy—the Right Hand of Allah, but the right hand of what did most good, which to the Bedouin was about the same. In fact, Frukey had done a great deal in the forty or more years he had been there. His daily medical patrol brought in many a woman in painful childbirth, many a child burned or scalded, many a man hurt in hunting or the accidents of his business, not least the chewing bite of a camel, the lunge of a horse, or what was worst, venereal disease so far as tertiary syphilis. Long before he had agreed with the Emir's father to build a special hospital with male orderlies to take care of all those cases, realizing it was unfair to the nuns to thrust that care onto them, because they would have to handle and cleanse male genitals. As it happened, those orderlies were not properly trained and the nuns had to be called in, and, as ever, they rectified a horror.

'Look,' Frukey said to me once, with his fists on his desk. 'You have got to realize that these nuns have given their lives to Christ. Never mind what you think, that is the fact. What does it mean? They live on a different level from you. A *different* level. Higher, if you like. Or nowhere if you think otherwise. Fact is, they can do a lot more than you can. Or the rest of us can. How? Prayer. They're always on their knees, begging for this, that, and the other. Things we don't even think about. But generally they come to pass. That's the wonder. How?'

'They don't live as we do,' I said. 'We have to do as we must. They do as they wish. Between wishing and doing is a hell of a difference!'

'Correct,' Frukey said. 'But remember. We do as we want because we think so. We *think*. Are we right? The nuns pray to the Lord God. He thinks *for* them. So they say. Who thinks for us?'

That was a puzzler for me. Who thinks for *us*? I suspect that Frukey always believed in the nuns' way. He always gave them all they wanted. They asked for a new operating theatre? They got it. They wanted a new playground for the girls and a football field for the boys? They got them. They wanted a new school because the

Bedouin were bringing in their children to learn? It was built. They wanted a nursing school to train Bedouin girls to take care of their own women? They got it? Frukey sent his nightly messages to BB in London, the next morning he had the answers, and within hours the surveyors and building teams were doing their jobs. I saw the work going on. I had never had any doubt that BB's way was the way to be. Get on with it. That was the way I was trained. I never knew any other.

I think we all grew up—or certainly I did—when the ice cream truck came in on a tanker's deck, and I can't for the life of me think why, except that the sight of its white enamel and blue lettering—UM'M SHAM'MS ICE CREAMERY—made everything seem modernised in some way I would have found hard to explain.

'Bloody old fool!' Frukey said. 'Going into his dotage. What's the use of that here? Can't find enough milk for a decent cup of tea. Where're we going to find cream?'

But the girls and Fuad opened the interior to find cartons of concentrated cream and tins of flavourings and suddenly we all had plates of the best ice cream that ever was, and I think that life changed for the better if only because we seemed nearer to our own civilization. A plateful of ice cream seems little enough, though heaven knows what other reason there could have been. To see Fuad coming into the yard with a trail of Bedouin children all dancing for ice cream was a wonderful moment, and Frukey leaned out of his office window to shout that they should go to their tents on the hill with a bucketful, and the girls helped Fuad with chocolate and strawberry and vanilla, and the children went away singing, with Abd carrying the heavy bucket in one hand and holding the carton of cornets in the other.

7

WHEN I first got there in the mid-fifties, we were about a dozen all told, five Beirutis in accounts, four women secretaries, Frukey and myself and Ito, nicest of the nice, a Japanese engineer in charge of bunkerage. On a sad day, he was killed by a horned adder. The Bedouin came in to find and destroy the nest, and they did, and we never saw another. But I never forgot Frukey's grief, or what he said that awful night.

'Always have the place well searched by the Bedu,' he croaked, in mid-tumbler of Scotch. 'Never leave anything to chance. Here, we lose a first-class man by an error of judgment. *My* error. From now on, we need a couple of men on the watch for snakes, scorpions, and the rest. I suppose they have to live, too. But not here. See to it!'

From then on, we were the least infested area on the coast, and when the nuns heard about it, they wanted our help, and they got it. Abd said the place was crawling, but since snakeskins have a value, and scorpions in plastic make excellent paperweights, all turned out for the best. The soukhs took the benefit, and the nuns made the profit.

That first Easter was something of a mess, because the few captains got Frukey as helplessly drunk as themselves, and the luncheon went to waste. The secretaries and I dined off delicious sandwiches and fruit salad, and we drank a Retsina—the first taste I ever had, and one I love down to now—and the nuns carried off the prepared dishes for the orphans.

'This simply cannot be allowed to happen again,' Frukey said a few days later, lax and creased and hoarse. 'The staff is to be augmented. More women. We therefore have to be considerably more circumspect in what we do.'

'We did perfectly well, sir,' I said.

'Young man, when I want advice from you, I shall ask, though for the moment I see no opportunity. Kindly do as you're told and keep your mouth shut!'

'Why not have a room especially for the drinkers? Then the women won't hear or see them.'

'What did I— Wait a minute. That's a good idea. But where?'

'Up on the roof. Insulated. The noise goes wherever it goes. Not a sound below.'

'Splendid. Set about it soonest!'

I did, and we had two storeys on top of the original block, buttressed by steel and concrete, with a stairway from the outside, but enclosed in baulks of timber, so that if drunkards fell back, they would not fall out. And it looked good, with a flooring of parquet, waxed and shining, and in the lower room a bar with mirrors and polished barrels, long racks of crystal glasses and all the bottles there are, under the care of two famous barmen from Cairo. Of course, the captains spread the word, and soon the rooms were crowded, and the mates came to me and complained they had nowhere to go except Zazi's. After all, they had gold stripes on their tunics, too, and if captains could drink in privacy, then so should they.

'They're right, dammit,' Frukey said. 'They're the captains of the future. Call in those architects again. Build something as good for them. They're all good lads. We'll need them.'

And so the first mates and their juniors got their place, further along the roof but behind, toward the sea, and below, a library for those studying for a master's certificate and for men wanting to read in peace or write a letter home.

But when the new women were expected, we had another sort of problem. There were far more of them than I had thought. Business had grown almost as we watched, up to twice its former size, and it seemed to be

38

going to double that, and in the shortest time it did. More women secretaries joined us. In those months we had to call in the architects to build an entire women's quarter, with a swimming pool, sauna, gymnasium, library, and all the other designs architects can draw to let women feel they are being cared for. Um'm Sham'ms was transformed overnight. When the Carrara marble came in on the tankers, with the drawings pegged on the information boards in the main foyer, we knew what we were in for.

'It's going to be a bloody hotel,' Frukey said. 'The best between here and Karachi, but still a hotel. And don't think it's going to be easy to run. It could turn into a brothel. Not in *my* time! I'll get policewomen pensioners to supervise it to my directives. There won't be any boy friends. They can go up to Bahrein or anywhere else for that. Not here. And by the way, what's your idea of coming in my office dressed like that?'

The weather was hot, the air made everything ripple, and the air conditioners were turned off because of the builders. I had on a linen shirt and trousers, and they were soaked. Frukey wore a business suit, shirt and tie, and the shirt was starched stiff, collar and cuffs.

'In future,' he said, with a lot of frost, 'and I think I've told you before, you will dress for this office as you would for Head Office in Threadneedle Street. What do you think BB would say if he walked in here and saw you in this condition? In future you will dress correctly. Do you understand? We *are* in a bad way. But when we slacken discipline, we are infinitely worse off. Got that?'

'Sir.'

He opened a lower drawer in the desk.

'These are Hilsly's latest reports from Teheran,' he said. 'You should have seen them some time ago, but I thought they mightn't have made much of an impact. I was thinking of sending you up there. But when he lost

Louise, that lovely girl of his, he went on the bottle, and I didn't think it the place for you. Working with an alcoholic was never the place for a young man. BB agreed. Everything's getting worse up there. The natives are getting barbary. Don't like doing what they're told any more. This fellow Mossadegh preached poison all over the place, and a lot of them believed him. He was a nuisance. Glad he was got rid of. It's still the business world against Islamic-nationalist prejudice. But what the hell, the *people* are Islamic. They believe one way. We've got a different point of view. Business is banks, oil, insurance, the market and all that. Western stuff. Us, if you like. What's going to happen?'

'Sir, what do *you* think?'

'Don't know. But I don't think we'll be here very long, and that's certain!'

'Then what are we building for?'

'To lodge the staff we need. After that, barracks. BB's a wise old bird. He'll get his money back, don't worry!'

Frukey saw my doubt.

'Look,' he said. 'It's about time you grew up.'

He went over to the big wall map of Iran, showing all the regions and the principal cities, and dotted his fore-finger on Teheran.

'That's somewhere about six hundred miles from this coast, without any roads. Just tracks. It's pretty well desert. If there happens to be a blow-up, how d'you get troops from the coast to there? Fly 'em? No airfields. Where are the docks. Have a look up and down this coast. What have you got except oil tanks and bunkerage? Where would a navy land troops? How long would it take engineers to build the facilities? Months? How would you supply the troops? Don't bother. It's really not on. Worse than that, these people can sling us out any time they like. What defence have we?'

'Well. We could send in a few gunboats?'

'Across six hundred miles of sand?'

'Hasn't anybody thought about it?'

'Possibly. But the cost might reach hundreds of millions. How many politicians want to think about it?'

'Isn't there *any*thing we could do?'

'Mossadegh was a fairly foxy sort of lad. If he had put a tourniquet on the oil flow, what could we have done?'

'Not much?'

'I'm afraid you're right. Not much. Politicians have no eyes for the future. Today, tomorrow, and the voters at home. To hell with the future! Isn't that it?'

8

WEDNESDAY MORNING and a freezing dawn, I remember, when the first girls came in from Hong Kong, Singapore, Colombo, Bombay and Karachi, and the men lifted them out of the boats to follow Abd up the beach—ghosts in the blurring mist—and I went down to check their baggage against my list. One bag was missing, so I had to go out to the tanker to find it. I went up the rope ladder, and there the crocodile bag was. In the scuppers. I knew how deckhands made extra money. That bag and its contents would have given them all a nice makeweight to their pay. I never trusted crews after that. I always went aboard when girls came in and checked the crane-loads. No more bags ever went missing. I don't know why I called them girls. They were all older than me, all of them had far more experience in company business, and they were there to take complete charge of tanker traffic between their home ports and us, and the onward traffic

41

to the Mediterranean, Europe, the United States and Japan.

Upstairs, I took the bag from Fuad and pressed the bell.

Ranina Sonakris opened the door, and her eyes and mouth went to O's. I put the bag down to ask a question, but she opened her arms and took me close, and I felt the hardness of her breasts, and she kissed me in what sounded like a long suck. She wanted to pull me in, but Fuad tapped me on the shoulder. Frukey was right behind me.

'Come with me, young fella,' he said, and looked at Miss Sonakris. 'Don't unpack. You're going to Alexandria. This evening. Be ready!'

I have never forgotten her look at me, and her imprint is still upon me. The bones of her thighs, the sweet nothing of her waist, her warmth through the silken wrap, and the unknown—until then—wonder of a woman's kiss. Of course, I thought of all that sort of thing with the steamy pseudo-poetry of the adolescent, and there was nothing wrong with it. But I think it a shame, when geriatrics pretend to be giving good advice while, really, they are simply being spoilsport horses' arses. I wish I'd known it then. But, after all, Frukey was boss and that was that.

I went out to fish that afternoon, and when I came back her tanker was on the skyline.

I shall never forget how I felt. I'd had a real hard from the moment I left her. A hard is something a lad has to live with, and though I don't know about others, it certainly lived with *me*. It hurt like the devil, too, which of course led to my looking at other girls with a feeling almost as sharp as hunger, which I came to know later had its own name, set forth in the Bible as a sin. Lust.

That word sounded very good to me.

When I knew what it meant, I ran it over and over my

tongue, thinking of women without knowing why, but remembering, I suppose, Ranina almost every moment. Strange, how a girl can perfume a life far beyond any memory of how she looked or the sound of her voice. It's odd that you can 'feel' a girl without remembering her or very much about her. But you do. She's stuck in your mind, the nicest thought you will ever know. All other girls will have to race that—at best—tenuous gauntlet, so often to fail, always without knowing about that tanker on the skyline or anything remotely to do with it.

I had a job in the filing room, a big place under Frukey's office, corridors of files up and down, with a wheel-ladder to reach the top rows, and I was almost at the top when Mrs Pincus came in, settled a few files, and came to stand beneath me, looking up.

'You never have much fun, do you?' she whispered, on my way down, and to my amazement her hand was on the bump in my trousers. 'Ooh, I could do with this. How about a bit of nooky?'

She opened my trousers and took him out.

'Half a mo'!' she said, and ran across to slide the bolt on the door, coming back, taking off the linen dress and putting two fingers down each side of her thighs to drop her panties on the floor. I suppose she was in her mid-twenties, slim and white, small nipples that seemed to want to stand up, and a candytuft of glinting curls that mesmerised me.

She pulled the quilt that covered the parchment documents from damp, threw it on the floor, and lay down, a Venus holding out her arms, and in moments of tearing off clothing I was sliding into the rooms of paradise to a music that ended in a thundering rain of unheard drums and the high sweet note of a violin, and began again, and once more the high sweet note, and again, and Mrs Pincus dropped her arms.

'I should have known about you before,' she said. 'A

43

lot of us can do with a bit of this. Wait till they know we've got a dyed-in-the-wool billycock, no less, kicking up his hooves on the sacred premises. They'll be queued up. Would you mind that?'

I shook my head, and she rolled from under.

'That's saved my life,' she said. 'All you want's a couple of lessons. This your first time?'

I nodded.

'Lovely to know I had a virgin. That's how it felt. Did you like it?'

'Loved it!'

'Nothing like it when you really want it. Phew! You took it out of me. You feel all right?'

'Marvellous!'

'Fine. Now, go to the bathroom and give yourself a good wash, with soap. Never forget that. You can't learn a good habit too soon. I'm very particular. A lot of girls aren't. They can give you a dose of clap or something worse. Remember that. Doesn't matter who you've been with, wash. That's the first rule. Listening? Right, off you go!'

So I trousered and the rest, and kissed her because she held up her face, and caressed her breasts, and went over to slide the bolt and go upstairs to my place for the wash.

But when I met her in the afternoon, she looked right through me. I exchanged sheets with her, she stamped them, and that was all. I was left feeling like a mug. But I quickly realized that her way meant no trouble with Frukey or anyone else. Under the carpet and keep quiet.

It went on for a little while, I suppose a few days, and then Wendy Lawes pulled my jacket one morning as I passed her desk with the transit vouchers.

'How about coming to see me in my room?' she whispered.

I nodded.

'Number twelve. Four-thirty?'

I nodded again, and she smiled and blinked and went back to typing.

At four-fifteen there I was, and at four-sixteen or not long after, I was in bed with a real beauty, although before I might not have given her a vote. Clothing detracts. It drapes or covers a figure, whereas naked, the girl or woman becomes at times ethereal, not even of the world round about, but a glorious somebody apart.

I learned that afternoon with Wendy Lawes. She was simply beautiful, a marvellous girl, and we went almost to six on the bell, which meant we had thirty minutes to reach our desks for the night shift, but we could have gone on without any trouble, and she put me in her mouth.

'Don't forget me in the rush,' she said. 'I need it. We *all* do. But we don't like the sailors here. They go to all the whoreshops. Pick up an infection, and then where are you? Down at the hospital and sacked. Not worth it. We prefer a lovely rod all our own. And you've got a lovely rod. No doubt about it. Short and thick, that does the trick. Put him in again. Ahhh! There I go. It's marvellous!'

She went naked to the door and bent to look up and down, and nodded, and I zipped my trousers, bent to kiss her lovely rump, both cheeks, and ran down the corridor and up the stairs to my place and the bathroom.

That darling girl, Marta van der Hooft, went with me to Bahrein one Sunday and, although I had no reason to believe that we would share a room—in fact, a suite— I had no complaint. She was tall, slim, and I wish there were any other word, Dutch. She was wonderful, white, seemingly cool until she was in bed, and her red-and-gold spun-sugar whirl really enchanted.

I was beginning to learn about women. I am so glad I had that long season with those voracious beauties. I had

45

time to acknowledge my debt to *la tendresse*, the gentleness, the beauty of women.

If I had been asked which I would marry, I could never have answered. To me, they were all exquisite. But a lot of them were more than ten years older, and that makes a difference.

I really did not know the difference until Marta came on the tanker with me to Bahrein. She booked the passages because she had that desk, and of course the hotel. It all went marvellously, because of a howling sandstorm outside, which meant we took the afternoon and early evening off in bed, and when we went down to the restaurant, there were the two Japanese girls at a lonely table, so we hied them over, and got the champagne pouring, and that brought Prince Hassan across, a very nice man and one of the richest. After all, he owned the hotel.

'Well,' he said, bending behind Marta's chair. 'You entertain these lovely girls and do not invite me?'

'I didn't know you were here,' I said. 'Pull up a chair and share a glass. The Prince Hassan—he has many more names—Miss van der Hooft—'

'Never mind, never mind!' the Prince said, in a wave of bediamonded hands. 'Names are a nuisance. Call me Jake!'

'Jakey-wakey!' we all toasted, and drank, and the Prince ordered a magnum, which was not at all on my shopping list.

'Sir,' I said. 'I am the host at this table. It is my duty to pay for my guests, including your good self. I cannot permit you to pay for a magnum. That is *my* privilege!'

The prince put his tongue down in his lower gum, opened his mouth, and laughed shut-eyed at the ceiling.

'Very well, dear Jon!' he said. 'By all means pay for the magnum. It will have a better taste!'

'We insist on paying our share!' Toshi said.

46

'Not permitted. Even I'm not. Jon's a bit of a boss. I like it!' said Marta, with a smile for me.

But when I went down to reception at dawn to catch the first flight, the cashier said there was no record of my stay, or any restaurant account.

That nettled me. When I got back to the office at Um'm Sham'ms I got the figures from Marta's booking, and she got the price of five dinners, a magnum and a bottle of champagne, and two bottles of wine, and I added a good tip and sent it to the hotel. Two days later I had a call from the Prince.

'You are a naughty boy, dear Jon. When I offer a hospitality I do not expect it to be thrown in my face. But I understand and I accept your principles. It is something to meet a principled man in these days. I have accepted your cheque with thanks, and I wish to invite you and the same guests on the last day of this month. I shall look forward to meeting you. I am your friend. You know?'

The secretary put the phone down in a giggle. It sounded pretty.

'I hear you had a fine time in the company of the Prince Hassan,' Frukey said, when I took the morning report to his office. 'That's expensive company, isn't it?'

'Sir,' I said.

'Don't do too much of it. You've got a healthy bank balance, but it won't last long if you entertain men like him. Has he ever asked you any questions about what goes on here? Oil returns, etcetera?'

'Never. I doubt he would.'

'Be very careful. Any scrap of intelligence goes to the boys upstairs. They're a sharp lot. Why not? Oxford, Cambridge, Harvard, all that. We're stuck in a nation that's neurosis-prone. They're not like the Bedu. They're half-village, half-big-town-sewage wallahs. For them, their big town is the big world. They've *even* got four-storey houses! And apartment buildings going up to the sky. And washing machines and refrigerators. They're still a rough lot of allsorts. Sunnis, Shi'ites, anything you like.'

'Do you think they want to shift us, sir?'

'Of course. They think they can handle the business just as well as we can. And make more money without us. How long do we last?'

'But I wouldn't want to leave here, sir. It doesn't seem fair, does it?'

'Fair is as fair does, but needs must, etcetera. And you know what beats me? It was all ours only a few years ago. We could have hung on to all of it.'

'Well, why *didn't* we?'

'Purblind bloody politicians, lad, that's all. We tried to tell them. BB planned it for them. I mean, the alternative. Let India have independence. It was always a burden on us. Transfer the Indian Army to stations in Persia, Iraq, and Saudi Arabia. We could have held, and to spare. But no. They couldn't see even as far as their noses. Maps? They weren't looking. Do you know that some of them didn't even know what *Islam* was?'

'Can't mean that, sir?'

'Mean it? 'Course I mean it. Go and ask some of them now. What *is* Islam? Probably think it was some new type of soap powder. Bloody lot of idiots!'

9

DAYS, WEEKS, months passed, and all went on the same, and had I not seen the date stamps on the paperwork, even years would have seemed the same, until the morning I came back from a falcon hunt. As I gave my beautiful mare to the stable lad, he told me that Frukey had fallen down the stairs and broken a leg. I ran for Mrs Pincus and found her in the tearoom, still swollen about the eyes, and crying again as she told me of his flight to Bahrein and onward to London, and a Harley Street clinic.

'Nicest man in this world,' she said. 'I had nigh ten years with him. Never a word out of place, me or anybody else. A gentleman, fair and square. Very strict, yes. But he knew where he was, and what was going on. He thought you were the high-olly-cocko with a run of the barnyard. He didn't mind as long as it didn't affect the work. In fact, he thought it was healthy. There's all sorts of appetites. All got to be served one way or another. He thought you satisfied a—he called it—a gentle demand. I said you did, and I'd been one of the first. That made him laugh. Oh, he *did* laugh!'

'You didn't mind telling him?'

'Certainly not. I believe *his* way. Be honest. Then nobody can catch you out. Can't say you're sly or underhand. This is *me*. I've done so-and-so. What about it?'

'I don't think I could have done it. Being honest, I mean.'

'Why not? You were honest enough to take your trousers off. Why not the rest?'

'Well, doing something and talking about it's two different things, isn't it?'

'Is it? D'you feel like it now?'

'Yes.'

'Come on, then. I'm feeling like it, too. Straighten me up.'

It had taken me a while to find out that Mrs Pincus was not only beautiful but a darling woman. I didn't then know enough *about* women. I had simply been thrown among a lot of the hungry at a time when I knew

49

nothing about them or myself. It was too easy to put the lad into a lovely warm cleft and keep going, and when I felt their response and heard their sounds, they seemed to rouse a savagery in me that it took a little time to understand and control, and there again Mrs Pincus helped.

'Listen, Jon,' she said, that afternoon with her arms still about me. 'You're growing up. Y'getting stronger. That's lovely. Only don't treat us like lumps of meat. We're not. We love it as much as you do, but we like to feel there's a little bit of love there, too. Else what's the use? A lot of the girls are going on this Lesbian kick. I don't hold with it, but that's not to say they haven't the right to do what they want. Listen, let me tell you a story. My husband was a bastard. He gave me a dose of clap—'

I kissed her on the shoulder.

'First mistake I made, I went to our family doctor. *I* hadn't any idea what it was. He did, and he told my father. Well, I got kicked out. I was no more family of his. My father was that sort. So I went to hospital and got the injections until I was clean. But I couldn't stand London any more. I hated it. I got a divorce. I went to a private employment agency and asked for any job, anywhere. That's when I came here. Five times what I could earn anywhere else. My own quarters and two servants. Sounded marvellous. Been here ever since. Go round the other girls. You'll get the same story, more or less. What makes a woman come out here to this bloody godforsaken place? I'll tell you. She wants to be on her own, away from all the other stuff. I hate thinking of going back!'

'Any chance?'

'Frukey's broken his leg, and it wasn't a simple fracture. Y'think BB'll let him come back? He's been in line for a pension for a long time. Only reason he was

50

here this long's that he was the best, and BB's generation. This isn't a very important place any more, either. Khargh up the coast's been getting a lot bigger. But they haven't got the staff we do. Arabs. They don't employ women. More fools them. I expect Hilsly'll come down from Teheran. Little while longer, we'll *all* get the shove. We won't have this lovely life any more. Come on, fuck me. *Fuck* me. What else have I got?'

I heard that frenetic whisper all the way down the stairs, and the curious thing is that I never knew her first name. I still think it extraordinary that a man may enjoy the deepest intimacy of a woman's life and revel in her passion and yet not know her name.

BB's secretary, Mrs Maude Bailey-Hyde, called twice to say that Frukey was quite comfortable and that he was sure I could control everything that went on, and to expect Mr Hilsly in the next couple of days.

He came in at seven in the morning, a big man with a big voice and a deliberate way of walking, but we were all at work and nothing out of place. He looked through the paper, stuck the pen in the holder, and looked up at me.

'I think you're capable of running this place,' he said. 'I don't think we need a replacement. You're only twenty-one, but you've had Frukey's training and you've got the best staff out here. That's what matters. Any problems?'

'Only the threats from the other side.'

'Mmmh. The job across the water? The Emirates?'

'No. Behind us. We're in a bad way. Arabs against the rest.'

'Same old story. Lucky we've got the mountains.'

'Mister Hilsly, do you think they'll ever kick us out?'

'Not while the Shah's got an army. 'Sides, how long'd they last? They're an idle bloody lot, y'know. I couldn't trust production to the single best man on my staff. Be like handing it over to an infant. No, for the moment we're safe enough.'

'Doesn't sound too promising, though.'

'Nothing does anywhere around here. It's *all* dicey. The worst time in my experience, and that's not so much longer than yours, is it? Nervy. Well, that's enough of that. From what I've seen, you're quite capable of controlling this terminal, and I'll tell BB so tonight. You're doing a great job. Keep it up!'

I saw him away in the helicopter for Bahrein, and went back to the office to open the package he had left on the desk. It was a detailed evacuation plan for the entire office staff, myself included, to fly up to Bahrein and on to Rome, where the women would be redirected wherever they wished, and I would proceed to London.

Any notion of it made me feel weak. For some stupid reason the strength went out of my knees. I simply did not want to leave Um'm Sham'ms. The thought of living anywhere else struck panic deep in my gut. Even the prospect of a sail in Khalil's yacht lost any taste. I waved to Huq to dock her, shut the window, and went upstairs to the buffet—probably the luckiest walk I ever took.

Five princely brothers and the Emir sat at Frukey's round table, all in Arab dress. The Emir's hand patted the chair beside him.

'Dear Jon, we had hoped to meet you,' he said. 'I shall speak in Arabic because I am sure you understand. I leave these papers here for later study. I wish to say that the bankers here are all a stupefaction in concrete. They have little idea what to do with an excess of money. But we are fathers of families and we want to safeguard our future. Oil will be gone someday. It is time to think of capital investment on a much bigger scale. My brothers and I control billions in every currency. It should work correctly instead of remaining figures on a balance sheet

52

that rises day by day. Every time I see those figures I wonder if I'm sane. The bankers see them merely as a source of profit. Any sum lodged with them simply enlarges their area of profit. It does little for us. I have my family and my people to think about.'

He put the packet on the table in front of me.

'I asked a systems firm to make a reconnaissance,' he said. 'That report is their finding. I am disappointed with it. It is a report written by men of a past generation. But you see, Khalil and yourself are men of a newer age. With other ideas. I prefer to listen to you. You will live and direct in *that* world. *Your* world. You see?'

I nodded. I had no idea of what was coming next.

The other faces were blank, though alive to listen.

'You have proved your worth at this terminal,' the Emir went on. 'I spoke with Mister Fruark last night at his hospital in London. He is much better, but he will not be coming back. You are going to be in charge here. This suits me perfectly. When Khalil has finished with his military training, he will come back here. He and the sons of my brothers will form a partnership with you. We have decided this because you have the business sense, and none of them have. You agree?'

'I still have a contract with Mister Blount?'

The hand waved and the rest nodded.

'That can be arranged,' the Emir said, and again the rest nodded. 'All we wish to do at this meeting is to be assured that you agree to our proposal. All terms and incidentals to be settled at a later date. You have objections?'

What was the use of objecting?

'No, sir,' I said. 'I shall enjoy working with the Prince Khalil. He's a smart lad!'

'I am happy to hear you say so. You will read the report and let me have your opinion?

'By tomorrow afternoon, sir.'

'I shall expect you at five o'clock. Now, a little cup of coffee, and we shall go.'

I was on the telephone to Frukey that night, and I told him of the meeting.

'Excellent!' he said. 'Go after it. The pair of you could make a big difference, especially with the others putting their shoulders to it. The princes are a hard lot, y'know. Nothing soft about them. If they make a decision, that's it. There's no going back. Be just the same with their sons. Don't forget there's a billion now, billions next year, and the year after that as far as I can see. I'm talking about *billions*, not millions. Hear the difference?'

'I do!'

'Play your cards, son. Always be on their side. You can always rely on a fair deal. Arabs are honourable. I've always found them so. I've never known one to go back on his word. Never. So treat this very seriously. You're in good hands. When are you seeing BB?'

'I haven't heard anything yet.'

'He's ill, that's why. He'll be on to you shortly. Call me whenever you like. How are the girls?'

'They're fine. Working hard, of course.'

'Always did. Y'know, if you think about it, women are marvellous. All of them. Out there, yes, they can go wherever they wish, all very well. But they're still far from home. It's alien country. It's going to fall on top of us soon. I don't like to think of my girls in a state of worry. They don't deserve it.'

'Won't happen if I can help it!'

'Good. Keep going, son. You're doing fine!'

But that talk was far from satisfying.

I had a feeling something was happening somewhere that I should know more about, but I had no notion what it could be, and though I might pull my brain out of shape, not a hint took form and not even a word crept through. Still, I wondered why Frukey had called me son.

He had never done it before. In all the time I had known him, he was never more than correct, almost icily so. Why the new warmth? Son, in Frukey's mouth, was something of a different order, almost unbelievable unless I had mistaken what I heard. I had not, and it troubled me.

I took that trouble into the reading of the Emir's proposal, a simple enough outline of what he intended. The amount of money was never mentioned, but at the back of my head I heard Frukey's voice talking about billions. I wrote a sequence of notes and Mrs Pincus typed them for me, and I presented myself at the Palace that afternoon at a few minutes before five o'clock.

As well I did.

I met M'aroukh.

10

I WALKED through the main entrance into the hall, and all the lights were switched on, and she stood under a huge chandelier looking at me, the loveliest woman I had ever seen or imagined, and from that moment any thought of other women was cleansed from my mind.

It was a moment to realize.

I knew I had fallen in love.

Love.

The word I had heard all my life, in what little poetry I had read, in song-lyrics, doggerel, and novels. The meaning had never got into my head. But then, at that precise moment, I knew what it meant. But to put it into words?

I stood there under the lights looking at her.

She wore a shift of Arab cotton from the looms of Bedu women, a creamy colour, beautifully draped, outlining breasts and pelvis but never in detail, merely demarking—with subtle emphasis—the loveliness beneath. Eve was exposed without any exposure, except to the prying eye and the prurient mind, and I had neither.

The major-domo announced me, and the Emir came out in Arab dress with a gold knife on a gold belt.

It had all taken a few seconds, though to me it seemed years.

'Ah, Jonathan!' the Emir said. 'So glad you are here. This is my eldest daughter, M'aroukh. Mister Jonathan Tewkes, whom you've heard about.'

'Indeed!' she said. 'Almost too much!'

'But, my darling, isn't that very rude?' the Emir said, looking surprised. 'Your Cambridge manners are showing, surely?'

'Possibly, but it was Oxford, actually!'

'Ah, yes. I always get them mixed up. There's not much difference, is there?'

'Whisper it not in Gath!' she said, and laughed, a beautiful sound, and I realized that she spoke perfect English without the smallest accent. She also had the loveliest grey eyes, probably a gift from a Berber ancestor, and a hint of red in her hair that was not of henna.

'Come in,' the Emir said. 'You read the report?'

'I did. I have certain reservations.'

'I expected it. What are they?'

'This is my report. What's this about a woman on the committee?'

'My daughter you just met. She has been to the Harvard business school. You agree?'

'Agree!'

'Then I shall read your report and come over to you

56

tomorrow at five. My daughter would like to use the yacht. She may?'

'Naturally!'

'She will take her entourage. Eight people and four bodyguards. You object?'

'But, sir, of course not!'

'Good. You will send the yacht here at four o'clock. She will come across to meet you. You will have fishing tackle ready?'

'Of course. And I shall meet you at five.'

But he never got there. His troops had repelled an attack by his northern neighbours, and I was stuck with a fishing jaunt that I wanted—with all my heart—but Huq's frown and tiny shakes of the head implied an urgency, and the yacht left without me, possibly because I remembered Frukey's warning to stay away from Arabian women. But it gave me no hope in my struggle with thoughts of M'aroukh, that vision. She occluded me, shut me from light. Deep inside—where, I never could tell—I knew it was hopeless. But the more I knew, the more I wanted, and the longer I hoped. Hope. What a replete nonsense! It subsists on nothing more than imagination, and it dies as autumn leaves floating.

I sank to the level of the sad, the denied and neglected, a case of puppy-love gone scatterbrained. And all that for what?

A girl.

But *such* a girl. Stupid way to say the sweet fact. I went on for days in a fumble of imagination and the bare items of the office accounts, balance sheets, manifests, though whatever I looked at I saw her face, her beauty. What *is* beauty? After all, a lover's catalogue will express his feelings, but will it illustrate a fact, one to be accepted by the outsider? Does it affect the lover or erode his desire? Because desire is what it most certainly is, and trying to disguise it makes of a lover a thorough-paced

57

hypocrite. I did not want to be anything of the kind, but Frukey's advice and the tiny shakes of Huq's head were stringent warnings of direst trouble in the offing.

Mrs Pincus put a hand on my back as we walked down the corridor to accounts.

'What's been happening to you lately?' she whispered. 'Lots of lovely orgasms waiting to happen, and that includes mine, and you know what those are like, don't you? And I've felt yours, and I love them, and I'd like a lot more. What about it?'

'Any time.'

'Lovely. Meet you in my room after I've franked these accounts. All right? And I'll tell the girls you're out of the halter. Did you fuck her?'

An idea so gross really sickened me.

'No. And it's not the sort of word to be used in that connection!'

'Come off it! D'you want me to say "did you indulge in sexual intercourse"? We're living today, y'know. What I said's what we do. It's a lovely word, I think. It says what it means. It doesn't play about. Expect you about four-thirty, all right?'

I nodded, without the courage or smallest ability to tell her that any thought of touching her disgusted me. But faced with an avid naked woman, the mind changes in the most extraordinary way, and in her own job Mrs Pincus was quite lovely. She loved what her body gave her, and so it was more than an hour's rabid excitement later that the office bell rang for resumption of work, and we got into clothing and chased out to our desks.

In the late evening, she came in with the day's work and we went through it, and I signed.

'That's fine,' she said, still a little red-eyed. 'Now I've got something a bit more important. You know Mollie Dovacos?'

'The big girl dealing with Greece?'

'That's the one. She's upsetting a lot of the others.'

'In what way?'

'She's been giving the eye to the Emir's guards, down there. And she's holding these *parties.*'

'Parties?'

'I was just told by the girl on the Turkish desk. She said there's a rotten atmosphere. It's getting like a nest. Y'know? Girls 'n' girls. I *said* it would happen!'

I thought for a moment, wondering how Frukey might have handled it, and I knew.

'Warn Miss Dovacos to get her stuff together, go to the cashier, take her travel allowance, and a ticket to London. I want her out within the hour. Report to me when she's gone. But you know, what we do isn't much better, is it?'

She looked down at me and smiled such a nice smile.

'What *we* do's healthy, *isn't* it?' she said, almost in a whisper. 'Least, *I* think so!'

11

I HEARD shouting down at the guardhouse and went out to the verandah to look along the courtyard and saw the Emir shouting at his troops, but I was too far away to hear, though I knew he was angry. I called Mrs Pincus on radiocom to warn her and the entire office of his arrival, and as I finished the call Ibn announced him.

He had a deep-copper tan and his uniform was unusually crumpled, so that I knew he had come direct from the front.

'Good morning, Jon,' he said, and held out a hand.

'We've had a remarkably sticky go up there, but we gave them the beating of a lifetime, with, of course, God's help!'

'A cup of tea, sir?'

'I'm parched. Since I'm on neutral ground, you could make that a glass of beer?'

'How about a glass of cold champagne?'

'I'm delighted you mentioned it. Yes!'

I made a sign and Ibn went away.

'There are two matters that have no connection. One, a certain member of your staff here's been trying to entice my guards—'

'I found out about it and sent her away that day. I doubt it will happen again!'

'Excellent! Mister Fruark had to deal with many cases and he dealt with them all the same way. Of course, these desert soldiers are handsome and these girls are not in clausura. Sometimes human nature has to be satisfied. I prefer it shall not be with my soldiers, d'you see? It gives them unhealthy ideas, and then I might have to shoot them. The second matter is more important. My daughter M'aroukh is determined to use her business skills in the oil business, and she would like to start here.'

'Now?'

'Exactly. She can go home every night in complete safety. She'll have her maids and guards with her. You agree?'

'Naturally!'

Ibn poured us a glass, and the Emir stood in a toast.

'To her first day in business,' he said. 'I have you to thank. To my beautiful M'aroukh!'

'Amen,' I said, and meant it.

'You are not a religious man, Jonathan?'

'Just enough to pray when I'm in trouble, sir.'

'Exactly the same as the rest of us!'

I nodded to Ibn and he refilled the glasses.

'How is Mister Fruark?' the Emir asked. 'He was such a nice man. Very trustworthy.'

'He's enjoying retirement, sir. His garden absorbs him.'

'Mister Blount?'

'Sir, I think from what he sends here, he hasn't the grip he once had.'

'It happens to all of us. Age. When does he go to grass?'

'I doubt he ever will. *Under* the grass, possibly. But for the moment, he's hanging on.'

'Any idea what Mister Fruark was worth? He was here for more than forty years. In the beginning, he was awarded two-and-a-half percent of oil, in and out. Later, rather more. Any idea?'

'None at all.'

'Any idea of the Blount fortune?'

'I never thought about it.'

He looked at the bubbles in his glass.

'You also are getting two-and-half percent on oil, in and out. That's a large sum. You never think of it?'

'Never, sir. I'm here. That's all.'

'You're a very unusual young man. You don't go on sprees and that sort of thing?'

'I go to Bahrein now and again.'

'Ah, well. Plenty of everything there. Which part of the building will you assign to M'aroukh?'

'I've been thinking about it. She can't go into the main room.'

'Why not?' he asked, in a flash of brown eyes.

I was stumped. I knew it. But an idea came.

'If she is to take control at some future time, she should not be thrown in with the people she must employ. She must be apart. I think the building must be enlarged. An upstairs office, and downstairs another filing room, which we badly need, and her own entrance.'

61

'Excellent. I shall send my architects tomorrow. My workmen will follow. I'm very pleased. Goodbye, dear Jon.'

I saw him away with every kind of mixed feeling. Delight that M'aroukh would be there every day, but despair that it could never lead to anything.

What are you to do when everything in the world is against you? Religion, family, race. Plus, that I had no idea how she thought, still less whether she had even noticed me. I sat at my desk and squeezed my shoulders together in a dried-blood cringe that I hoped might open up any sort of pathway to her. It was a prayer of sorts, I suppose, but certainly no man ever prayed harder for his love. I wonder if prayer to the Lord God is more efficient than prayer direct between the breasts of love. How is a man to define what a woman thinks? She is *her*self. He is *him*self. There is a terrifying gap between the two. Sitting across a table with a couple of drinks, it seems easy to bridge. But it never is.

It takes years of a thoroughly good marriage to accustom one to the other, and even then there are so many problems that marriages of twenty years come to nothing. I think it a most horrible tragedy. People's lives have been hollowed out. Both are defenceless. A woman's youth is gone. A husband's grasp is gone. What the devil have they to look forward to?

I clearly remember Frukey telling me that his divorce was a disastrous error which he regretted to the day.

'Never should have been allowed to happen,' he said. 'She was beautiful, intelligent, and gentle as the crocus in spring. Why did it happen? Very simple. I was stupid. I wanted her out here. At that time, this was mud huts. No aircraft anywhere. Nothing for her to do. I had a full day downstairs. She'd met a captain from one of the tankers, and that was that. Jon, if you ever get within marrying distance of a woman, make up your mind what you want to do for her, and after that for yourself. But never forget that the woman is the more important!'

He was drunk, but his words embedded. I never forgot them. That little place at that time was almost all I knew. All I had was his library, and I read everything, understanding very little but learning as the days went by. Then I went up to Bahrein for lessons in philosophy and all that, which—I regret—gave me a simple nothing. I could never understand what all the palaver was about. The Greeks and this and that and the other, very well, and Wittgenstein and all the rest in our day, all right, and what?

What?

They had resolved nothing.

Like the economists, they moiled in a burthen of words, without the smallest hope of an answer or—at any rate—one that might work. The only man who might have some of the right answers, it seemed to me, was Silvio Gesell, but there were not enough non-idiots to support his ideas, and the rest had never heard of him.

I can look out on the rest of the world and read the newspapers and journals, and listen to its radio and watch its television, but I have little hope that anything will be done to ameliorate the human condition. I never expected to hear anything of the sort from M'aroukh, but when she arrived to install herself and her staff in the new offices, we spoke of little else and I was given a lesson in the thinking of the Emirates and their Arabian compatriots.

They were quite sure that the Russians would try to cut the oil route to Europe.

'But, M'aroukh, what makes you think so?' I asked.

'My father and his brothers and most of our male relatives all trained in Europe or the United States in army or air force academies,' she said. 'They learned to look at maps. Maps tell a story. I was taught even as a child. We, here, are badly placed. A force across the land behind us, let's say, four or five times our numbers, and we're finished. The same for attack by sea from the south. We'd fight, but without hope of winning. Recuperation afterwards would be difficult. I think of the women and children. Their plight would be appalling. And you know? Who gives a damn?'

I looked at her, fresh as a flower in white linen.

'But surely the leaders here must have thought of all the consequences of attack? The aftermath?'

'Why should they. Most of them would be dead, or wounded so badly they could no longer fight. Why think of women and children? In times of peace they are family. In war, they are a nuisance. Isn't that so?'

'But why do you fight if it's not to protect your family?'

'That's a Western idea. We fight because someone pretends to be our master. We have only one master. He is enrolled in the Koran!'

'Do you believe it?'

'No!'

'Your father knows this?'

'Of course. We talk about little else. And my marriage.'

'Marriage?'

'He has a man of good family picked out. I simply cannot stand the sight of him. Any idea that he could touch me blasts every thought. I *will* not submit!'

'Where's this fellow now?'

She leaned forward in a smile.

'Are you going to shoot him, perhaps?' she said. 'How I would love that. My champion.'

As Frukey might have said, I was tooken aback.

'It hadn't occurred to me,' I told her, looking her in the eye. 'Why does your father wish you to marry a man you hate?'

'Inter-family relations. His family has enormous holdings. So has my father. The two together mean wealth and power. So? My father thinks the best way is to marry me to this misery. The families are linked. Our children inherit. That is the idea. I *won't*!'

'But you will?'

She turned away and nodded.

'I shall have to, or be killed. Unless some Lochinvar comes out of the west and pulls me onto his saddle and rides off. That would be nice!'

'I'm game,' I said. 'Couldn't we try it?'

'We would be dead within a couple of hours. I still don't think you understand the Arab way. Or the Arabs. Or my father. Or me. We can play with other ideas. We can pretend. But we can't cheat ourselves. We have nothing to do. We must obey!'

'Why?'

She shrugged and it bounced her breasts, tight, small.

'The Koran,' she said. 'Women are slaves. How many years until we fight free? It will depend on the mass of women in all the Arab countries. How *are* we to get together? There are millions of us. We can't. The men stop us. We are slaves. We must do as we are told. I *hate* it!'

'Same sort of battle's going on everywhere,' I said, for something to say.

'I went to a couple of meetings at Oxford. Marvellous enthusiasm. I saw what's being done in America. *I'd* like to make my own decisions. Perhaps my granddaughter will make hers, but I'll never have the smallest chance. Have you seen our women around here? If I suggested any of my ideas, I'd be stoned to death!'

'No!'

'Oh, yes. There's no moral fervour so vocal or poisonous as Islam's. It's a real chance for everybody to play the holier-than-thou. We are lunatics!'

'You're very hard on your own people?'

'I *know* us. I had almost five years away in England and America. I loved the freedom. I no longer had to ask advice, permission. I consulted my *self*. Then I came back here to the tenth century. Everything except the chains. Make a mistake and they throw stones until you are dead. You didn't know that?'

'I'd heard about it.'

'Now you know. And my father wouldn't lift a finger to stop it. It is the discipline of the Koran. Sharia. The law. Obey, or die. That's the effect!'

She had her back to me, looking out at the sea, and on impulse I went over to her and put my hands on her hips. She turned, a spitting wildcat, big eyes, claws.

'Take your *filthy* hands off me!' she breathed. 'Never come near me again. There is no need for you to enter this office. In future, keep out. Go!'

I went and, hearing the sounds of weeping, might have gone back.

But I shut the door.

12

THE RAINS began on a night I worked late. I turned on the heating system or else all the paper would have been sopping by morning. A time began when a cigarette could turn into green mould and a shirt would cling to you in the moisture of the air, not your own. No more falconing or polo, and no more fishing because the mist greyed sight, and tanker captains had to rely on electronics.

At first I had been sorry for the Bedu, but when I went up on the rise and called on Ibn, I found him in his black tent as warm as toast and not a bit worried about weeks of a fine drizzle. Big panniers of charcoal were set in various parts of the tent, and air vents in the roof took out the smoke. After all, they had been living there since time began, and they knew. It's something we are prone to ignore. People *know*, from their fathers and grandfathers. This or that works, and any nonsense about modernization simply does not. The heating plant at Um'm Sham'ms was the best of its kind, but we, too, went back to charcoal panniers and warmth, because that aged system worked. It gave warmth.

The only beacon in my life was Frukey's weekly telephone call via London. I gave him the daily figures, in and out, and he told me what went on in all the offices, and what BB thought of it, and what the newspapers were saying, and how many old ladies were being murdered, how the judges were dealing with the criminals, what was playing the theatres and cinemas, and what he was planting in his garden. It was a rubber stamp of our land, and I could see it as he said it, especially his flowers and what came out of his vast greenhouses. Then I could go back to Um'm Sham'ms and the comfort of braziers and the company of twenty-two women, not all of them with a claim on me, but just a few. They were getting more, though, and Marta van der Hooft warned me.

'You're the cock they want and they'll come on their knees for it,' she said. 'They're here for a couple of years. Don't forget that. A lot of the girls here are attracted to Sappho.'

'Lesbians?'

'That word is so over-used.'

'You're not attracted?'

She shook her head.

'I like men,' she said. 'The idea of making love to a woman even troubles my imagination. I *couldn't*. One day I shall marry and have children. How, with those memories? I'd want a man to give me his tongue. And then the rest. Women can only give themselves exquisite feelings. But so can men if they know enough. Too many can't. Why aren't they taught? Massage parlours. Ridiculous term. Masturbation horrors, better. It's very little for a prostitute to manhandle a man. Poor swine. And he pays? Poorer swine!'

'You better be careful,' Mrs Pincus said, that morning. 'Four girls in one day, that's the suicide rate. This way I get nothing!'

'There won't be any more for at least a week. I'm worn to the treads. Come in on Friday.'

'Sorry,' she said. 'That'll be the second day of my period. But I'll tell one of the Japanese girls instead. How's that?'

'Marvellous. I didn't know they were interested?'

'What do you think they are? Coffee urns?'

'Not exactly. But they've never shown the smallest interest.'

'They don't come from a nation that wears its heart on its sleeve. Besides, you're the boss here, and you've got plenty of your own women healthy and willing. Why *should* they?'

'Tell them any time!'

I began to think I was in charge of a meat shop, but in fact it most certainly was not. The girls made up their own minds. I never made an advance or gave any sign that I had a preference. Those beautiful Japanese bodies slipped through my hands as though oiled—fragrant, lithe and marvellous. If the truth were known, I preferred them to any of the others except Marta, my tall, exquisite goddess and—because of her wonderful passion—Mrs Pincus.

Toshi and Nobu were beautiful beyond expression, but in a curiously different way from the Europeans and others. They seemed to make a temple ceremony of the orgasm and all before. Going into them was a gentle groan and a pulling down of scented arms and rising thighs that stayed there so that I had nothing to do, and I heard that violin note and thunderous drums, and we began again, and delectable is hardly the word, though words are never the smallest use. I shall always remember them as the loveliest flowers of a lovely garden. They both went back to Osaka that year, but I was out with the falcons when the signal came through, and they boarded the tanker and were miles down the strait before I got back, and even then I knew nothing until Mrs Pincus told me.

'Never mind, darl',' she said. 'Plenty more where they came from. You've got more than enough here, haven't you?'

'That's not what I feel,' I said. 'I'll never see them again. But I'll always remember them. I wonder if they'll remember me?'

'I'd take a bet,' she said. 'They never did stop going to you, did they? Why? Because they didn't like you?'

'It's not that, y'know. I've been spoiled by a lot of lovely tender girls who wanted it and took it out on me. I've had a harem, if you like. I never deserved it. But losing two of the most beautiful hurts in a strange way. Even savagely. It all comes down to a question of what love is. A man can love two women or more, many more. People say it can't be done. I say it can. I'm the best judge. I love you, for example. I'd do anything for you. Anything at all!'

'Oh, you wouldn't!' she said. 'I don't believe it for a moment. I'm old enough to be your ma!'

'Don't sons love their mothers?'

'Of course. But they don't get into bed with them, do they?'

'We're off the track. Question of love, not bed.'

'So what's this I hear about motherfuckers?'

'Bad language. The worst possible. Probably out of the Negro ghetto.'

'Why Negro? Our own writers have written about it, haven't they? Anybody said anything?'

'Well, they'd keep it quiet. Church of England lot, Methodys, Baptists. Tread it all down, 'case they gave growing boys an idea. Double reason for loving them. Lots of mothers let their sons go in. Why not?'

'I don't like to think of it,' Mrs Pincus said. 'I could shudder!'

'Why?'

'Well, first of all, it's dead wrong. And next year I'll be going home. I'll be meeting a twenty-year-old son I love more than my life. If he gets ideas, how can I say no? I'm soft because of you. I've been a stupid mare. Wish I hadn't!'

She gathered the files and almost ran out.

The telephone was *rrr-rrr*ing next door and nobody answered. I had to get up and stop it.

'London, sir!' the operator said.

'Mister Blount's office,' the voice began. 'A message recorded ten minutes ago. It proceeds. "To my everlasting regret, my great good friend and colleague of fifty-eight years died in his sleep this morning. He is to be buried on Friday, and you will wish to attend. Your flights are booked for tomorrow. You will be met at Heathrow. Your suite here is booked. Your wreath for Mister Ranald Fruark has been ordered from Constance Spry. I shall look forward to dining with you. Until then." '

I felt myself plummet. Frukey, no longer with us? It seemed beyond imagining. But I knew I had to tell the staff. That was a matter of tears which I was unanxious to witness because I could join in. That was how I felt. I had lost a father.

I put my head in my arms and sobbed like an idiot.

I was able to wipe my face just before Miss Pearlman came in. She had been crying, too. But she should have gone to Mrs Pincus first.

'Well,' I said. 'What is it?'

'Sir, that man in accounts? He called me a dirty Jew bitch!' she said, and started to cry again.

I could almost feel Frukey standing beside me.

I reached out to press the button and waited.

Knocks, and Mrs Pincus came in.

'Who is this fellow in accounts who feels he may say what he pleases to my staff?' I asked her, and she looked at Miss Pearlman.

'He came last week from Rangoon, sir,' she said. 'I don't think you've met him. I don't think you'd want to. He's a nasty little two-face!'

'Let's be rid of both,' I said. 'Ask the cashier to give him travel money and his documents. He can take the tanker going to Alex this afternoon, and fly the slow way back to London. They'll give him his final pay there. I want him out in two hours. *Out*. Understood?'

Mrs Pincus touched Miss Pearlman's hand and they went to the door.

'I'll do that with pleasure!' she said. 'He made a few cracks at me, too. I think the Arabs have got a bit of a foothold?'

'Don't say that either!' I said. 'This is a business enterprise. There's no room for nonsense of that kind. Would you please remember that, and warn everybody else?'

Only a few minutes, and the door flew open to shake against the wall.

'I am Ammaus Rerong!' the man said, teeth bared and spittle flying. 'I am fifteen years with the company, and three years on Rangoon. You can't do it!'

'It's done. Leave!'

71

Ibn's arm came from the shadows and took him by the nape, swung him and threw him down the stairs. He laughed and I laughed, and he shut the door. I was told that Rerong's kit had been bundled into cartons, that he had been taken out to the tanker, still shouting, and that one of the mates had knocked him silly and put him in his bunk. That was that, and I was sorry. It did not seem to reflect any credit on us. To be thrown and punched was not our way. It was not Frukey's way. I had a notion that we had not heard the last of it. I have an instinct.

I buzzed for Mrs Pincus and told her I wished to address the whole staff in twenty minutes.

I told them as quickly as I could, and left them to their tears and sorrow. They had loved Frukey, too—and those who had not known him respected him for what he had achieved.

I wept again en route to London.

13

ARRIVING AT Heathrow, I was escorted to the car and was met by BB's secretary of many years. At the company hotel, a valet took us up to the suite and began unpacking for me. There was dismally little. I had nothing to go downstairs to dinner in. I had nothing for tomorrow morning except a linen suit, a shirt, yes, and a tie, yes?

'Oh, that's no problem,' Mrs Bailey-Hyde said, in a wave. 'Of course, you came in what you stood up in. Willis can take you to BB's tailors and haberdashers. All too simple!'

And it was.

I got back to the hotel after six, with a mass of packages that Willis took upstairs. I went into the bar for a drink, and met Greg Barrett from Singapore and Ian George from Colombo, my opposite numbers from those ports.

'Champagne cocktails!' Greg told the barman. 'This is an event. But not a very jolly one. I liked Frukey. I worked at Um'm Sham'ms before you got there. Best training I ever had. I wonder how long we'll last?'

'Who?' Ian asked.

'Us. All of us. Europe, if you like.'

'What can happen?'

'No oil, my friend!'

'Won't be allowed to happen,' I said.

'What'll stop it?' Ian asked.

'Combined forces.'

'Fighting a few thousand miles from their bases? It isn't on. The Russkis only have to go overland. Push through Iran from the north and the east from Afghanistan. On to Iraq and Syria. For them, nothing to it. They'll have the oil they want, plus several warm-water ports. Justification for guns instead of butter. We've got precious damn little to stop 'em. Here's to us. The losers!'

Ian knocked the glass out of Greg's hand.

'Don't you bloody well say that where I can hear it!' he said. 'They'd first of all have to deal with the Afghanis. It'd take a long time, and it'd bleed them. They'd have the same rough time in Iran and the rest. It'd be a battle of years. And the Chinese looking on? For how long till they saw an advantage?'

'We're all talking crystal balls,' I said. 'Let's leave it. Read any good girls lately?'

'Nip over to Rangoon and I'll show you the most beautiful,' Greg said. 'Then we'll go to Singapore and you'll tell me what you think. I'm not talking whores,

73

either. I'm going out later on a club-bash here. Why don't you two come? Get fixed up!'

'Not for me,' I said. 'I'm only too happy to take a couple of nights off.'

'Oh, Christ,' Greg said. 'An embarrassment of riches, eh?'

'Um'm Sham'ms?' Ian sighed. 'Always was. There was a marvellous black girl there. I tried to get her transferred to Colombo, but I couldn't remember her name. For heaven's sake!'

'A bloody fine Romeo,' Greg said, and raised a finger. 'Three more, please. What sort of tonnage you doing lately?'

'Oh, *no*!' Ian said. 'No you *don't*! God love Frukey every second, but I grabbed this to get away from the stench of oil and that bloody awful pile of paper. We got built in the wrong place. Every breath of wind blows in. Your clothing's stiff with it. I'm here for a clear couple of days to put a bunch of flowers on the old man and enjoy what he left me. Peace!'

It was a good note to say goodnight on.

14

THAT COUPLE of days in London, and the pilgrimage to Frukey's village taught me more about the state of our country than anything I had been able to garner from newspapers and journals. The place was dreary, and if far from cheap in price, then certainly in quality. I had the advantage of knowing Bahrein, where by then most of the best European shops had a window. In London, except for a few places, nothing approached them, and the few were very few. Bond Street was something of a desert, and Piccadilly was a real one, full of nothing, with the Circus a garish horror. Soho was a horrid market of female ploy, with a Chinese and Bangladeshi restaurant complex stretching for streets into the darkness beyond, and all the way back there were whores in doorways. Their whispers will follow me always.

I took a bus out to Barnet, to the two-storey suburbs, and looked at all those little houses and shops that had never grown and never would. I took a taxi back to Piccadilly, and left it on the corner of Regent Street.

I had entered another world. I could feel it.

I had once belonged to the two-storeys.

Now I belonged elsewhere.

I shuddered to think of going back to the two-storeys. I longed, I yearned for Um'm Sham'ms, my quiet suite and the ponies and falcons, and the whiff of oil here and there.

The porter gave me a message from Mrs Bailey-Hyde saying that whatever time I came in, to call her.

'Ah, yes,' she said. 'Would it be inconvenient to see him now?'

'Please!'

I went up to BB's suite, and walked into a wide drawing room redolent with vases of many kinds of flowers, rows of pictures on the walls, sculptures and silver pieces on all the tables.

BB sat in a scarlet padded dressing gown.

'Well!' he said. 'My favourite boy. I called you now because I have been sleeping all day. I wasn't at the funeral because I couldn't have borne it. I'm close to it myself. I'm older than he was. But, ah, I know you're off in the morning, and I wanted a couple of words with you. Frukey left you everything he had. You knew that?'

'No, sir.'

'Well, he did. It's a very great deal, including his property in the Cotswolds. You'll need an agent. Do you want me to find one?'

'Sir, if you would.'

'Very well. You will go back to Um'm Sham'ms to take charge not only of that wharfage but also of the other two. They are being combined under your control. Tanker captains have already been informed. You will therefore have more staff. Many of them will be Arabian, and—as you know—Arabians cannot work with women. It's against their law. Whether things will work as before, of course, we don't know. We can only try. So far as I'm concerned, I don't think we have much time there. Sad thing to say, but there it is. The top man, the Emir, I always found first-class. But he's under increasing attack. He can't go on. Neither can we, except to do our best for as long as we've got. It may be shorter than we hoped. Whatever it may be, we'll still be in the oil market, and with fair control. You began your tour after that one year at a half-percent on sales. You've since been at two-and-a-half, but from yesterday you're earning Frukey's five percent plus your own, making seven-point-five. Take the number of barrels at thirty-two dollars a barrel, and you'll see that you're a wealthy man. You still wish to go back to Um'm Sham'ms?'

'Nothing I want more, sir.'

'I'd hoped you'd say that. For one good reason. I've no idea who I'd put in your place. Have you any questions to ask me?'

'We need more accommodation, sir. We're cramped.'

'I'll talk to the Emir. Anything else?'

'I'd like an extra day to see the cottage, please, before going back.'

'Of course. We'll postpone your return by three days. Call in here for late documents and a last word, Frukey's going has affected me considerably, y'know? Did I say

76

I'm older than he was? You might find out what he died of. He always seemed remarkably healthy, at least to me. Well, I *feel* all right. About as much as I can expect, what? Go along with you, dear boy. See you before you go!'

Early next morning a chauffeur waited for me, and we went through clear sunlight into country I had never seen or dreamed about. This was, in fact, the England I had never known, and I suddenly understood the poets and songsters, and I knew why men would fight. I saw a glorious land of greenest fields and brown copses, and little brooks and rivers where I could almost smell the trout, and I saw houses and barns and gardens—all lovingly tended and cared-for—and I shall never forget the flowers in the hedgerows. I told the chauffeur to keep to the side roads, and so miss the asphalt miles of penitence on the main routes and I was more than repaid in another coin—by a greater joy in the real and not the artificial, and a wonder of herds pancaking the roads instead of giant trucks smoking their filth.

We got to Frukey's place by asking at the village pub, and we turned up a lane of honeysuckle to a gate, with a carved wooden label, 'The Cherish', and so it was.

Frukey had always told me that when he went back to England he would create a garden.

He had.

I never saw such colour. Paths, borders, beds were an amazing glow, strange to my eyes, welcome to my spirit, a delight in any terms, and I vowed then, in his memory, to keep it exactly as he had intended.

I stopped the car to meet a man, James Roberts, weeding in a wondrous bed of zinnias. I had seen him at the churchyard without knowing his name, but it took us no time to be on the best terms, and I knew I could trust him. Frukey was a judge of men.

He took me through the garden to the greenhouses,

four of them, fifty yards or more long, with orchids in one, and all the autumn plants ready for rooting.

'You'll take charge here and employ any extra help you need,' I said. 'Never be afraid. I'll back you to the hilt. Order what you wish. You're going to enter the horticultural show?'

'The Chelsea, sir? Ah, that was Mister Fruark's wish. Even to be *worthy* of showing. We're more than that, now, sir. We've got much better than a chance of winning in our class. The girls're certain of it. And, uh, sir, I don't like to talk about this, but they'd like a bit more money. Sorry to bring it up.'

'You were right to do so. Never be hesitant in talking to me. Double their pay immediately. That applies to you, too. Satisfactory?'

'Ah, sir, you don't know what you done. That's real marvellous. You'll see what happens. But there's er, well, it's er, sort-of, er—'

'Sort-of what?'

I looked at the lined red face, and all the seasons were there, stamped in the flesh of that magnificently strong English peasant's face, the grey-blue eyes restless as the sea itself, resolute.

'There's a bloke down the road there,' he said, doubtfully. 'Market gardener, he is. We've bought plants off of him. He's took a fancy to Fidelia, that's our top girl. She's miles above him. He makes her life a misery.'

'Why is he allowed in here?'

'Delivery of plants, sir.'

'Stop it!'

'They're paid for, sir.'

'Doesn't matter a damn. Cut him off. He no longer has the right to enter this property!'

'He's a dead rough bloke, sir. He's a big 'un. That's why the girls're afraid of him. See what I mean?'

'Why did you do business with him?'

'He knows his job, sir. He had the best plants.'

'Where is this Fidelia now?'

'Their half-day off. Be back tomorrow, eight o'clock.'

'What's the address of this swine?'

'It's in the village, sir. Ardville Close. Y'll see his name. Bensher.'

I asked him to take me down in the jeep, and away we went, to the village and a cul-de-sac with the nurseries on both sides green and thick, but unkempt.

Roberts stopped the jeep and shouted for Bensher. He came from one of the greenhouses, a tumbledown affair of broken glass and three-ply patches.

'This is Mister Tewkes, owner of The Cherish,' he said.

'Oh, ah?' Bensher grunted, and held out a hand.

'How many more plants are to come?' I asked him.

''Bout five thousand, I s'pose. Why?'

'Deliver them all tomorrow or I don't want them. Clear?'

'To*mor*row? That's impossible!'

'Get extra help and transport. I'll pay. But have it done. I don't want you anywhere near The Cherish after that. Understood?'

'But what's the idea?'

'You've made a nuisance of yourself with my women employees. I don't permit that sort of conduct. I want nothing more to do with you. If I have another complaint, I'll bring charges against you in the courts. Are you listening?'

He came toward me and I got out of the jeep. He *was* a big man, over six foot, and he was dark with anger.

'You're talking very big, ain't you?' he said. 'I give you a couple of minutes to get yourself off of *my* premises, else I'll deal with you!'

I had with me a cane I had bought in Alexandria, some strange wood many hundreds of years old, with a tube of

79

lead inside that made it heavy. I had gone through bayonet-training exercises with Khalil, and I had years of foil and sabre drill. People obviously did not know what they might be taking on.

He reached out for me, grabbed my lapels, and I realized his strength. I jabbed up with the stick and hit his Adam's apple, taking the skin off, and as he went back I swiped him over the left ear and came back to swipe the right, hard blows that sent him flat, no move.

'Better call an ambulance,' Roberts said. 'Bleedin' like a stuck pig.'

'His natural state. Call the ambulance, and we'll go. Those girls will never be bothered again. That's what's important. See that those plants reach us tomorrow, won't you?'

'I'll do that, sir. Depend on it!'

'I think I did enough damage?'

'He'll have a couple of cauliflower ears for the rest of his life. For pinching girls' backsides and squeezing their twatties. They should all be taken care of the same. But everybody don't have your guts, sir. He's a big bloke!'

'The bigger they are, the harder they fall. That's what Mister Fruark taught me. That's the finest man I'll ever know.'

'Sir, you're dead right. I could cry when I think of him!'

'It's been done, dear Roberts. I had to put my arms around more than twenty weeping girls. And they would *not* be comforted. He was a king among his own kind. I thought of him as my father. You know?'

'You're very much like him in your manner, sir. Direct. Y'don't mess about. You get what *you* want. And that's *it*.'

But the plants were not delivered, and I told our solicitors to take action.

15

I FLEW back to Bahrein, and took our helicopter on to Um'm Sham'ms, but to a vastly different staff. None of the old girls were there. Even Mrs Pincus had gone to take charge of the office in Piraeus. Marta van der Hooft was in Amsterdam. Only three women were at their desks. The rest were men, most in Arab head-dress, and one of them came to see me within a moment of my entering the office.

'We don't wish to serve with women,' he said. 'We hope you will take these women out and substitute men. We will give a list. They are ready.'

'My instructions come from London. Get out!'

Late that evening the Emir came in still wearing battle dress, and walked along my desk, a mountain of a man, and turned to look at me.

'The men here will be taken off at five o'clock each night, and they will be at their desks at seven-thirty in the morning,' he said. 'They will not work with women. You understand?'

'Understood, sir!'

'Further, you must consider the closure of this port!'

'Sir, we have a contract—'

'It can be abrogated!'

'London will have to decide, sir. I am merely an employee.'

'And so, you will do exactly as I tell you?'

'Sir?'

'Eighteen thousand barrels will go out instead of twenty. Your wharfage will go down to twelve. Next month, ten. The month after next Khalil will take charge here. I hope you will stay on to instruct him?'

'So that we have three months here at most? May I ask why this is happening? We had an agreement.'

He stood against the window, a massive black silhouette.

'In a nutshell, Arabia for the Arabians. I must fall in step. There has been great pressure recently. Iran is causing great trouble. There will be more. I cannot see any clearance there. How long have you been here?'

'A few months over eighteen years, sir.'

'Riding out with falcons, fishing, and supervising accounts etcetera. I don't think Khalil will require much instruction, do you?'

'He's smart enough.'

'I think so, too. I shall call Mister Blount tonight. To let him know. Your career will not end here, of course?'

'That's up to him, sir. He's still the boss.'

'Ah, but in his own company!' the Emir said. 'Not here, d'you see? This is my *land*, you see the difference? I am impelled by other influences. We need outside help in the technical details, but where we can control the day-to-day traffic, there we must accept our Arabian authority. So? I give you three months to leave this place, having first instructed my son in its management. You agree?'

'Sir, I haven't much of a choice, have I?'

He reached out and put a heavy hand on my shoulder.

'My son, you have served me excellently well. You shall have an excellent present, I assure you. Especially if you instruct Khalil to your level of efficiency.'

'It shall be done, sir. And if ever there's the slightest doubt, I'll come back and settle it, double-quick time!'

I saw him out to his helicopter and waved him off, though nobody ever felt less like waving.

I looked about the place. I loved every inch of it. All those miles of blue water out there. All the ochre-and-red mountains behind us. The stretches of desert I knew. The windblown trees we used as shelter and for firewood

82

when we roasted a breakfast. I went in to look at the falcons, and then to the stables to smooth and pat my mounts. They all knew me. They waited for their apples and whickered—that lovely sound—and kissed my face with wide, soft lips.

I understood the English word despair.

I had never had any real education, no proper schooling. All I knew was this patch of land, a few trips outside, most to Egypt and India, and from reading over the years those thousands of books in Frukey's library, with the newspapers and journals that came in every week and helped start the morning tea-fires to cook the bacon and eggs and, of course, the fish.

I would have to leave it.

Where was I to go?

To do what?

Despair is a good word. It would be nice to know who first thought of it. Some Anglo-Saxon who couldn't wrap his lips around *désespoir*, perhaps. But I felt like one of those unemployed in the queues in England, poor bastards. Nothing to do with marriage or illegitimacy, but with that other Norman-French word, *bâtard*.

Beyond the law.

I was with them, beyond the law.

A bastard.

Then, and for the first time in my life, I felt lonely and lost. I had never before felt alone. I had had plenty of friends all about me. Now, it seemed, I had none. There was BB, but after him, who?

That was a horribly grey evening, and while I toyed with dinner, the rains broke, gushing in curtains that rumbled thunder. Looking out of my window I could see nothing a yard away. But I was used to it, and I knew that within a month the entire desert to the horizon would bloom with grasses and lovely flowers that the girls so often ran out to pick for their desks, coming back soaked with their dresses stuck to them, a beautiful sight not to be missed.

The male staff had a terrible time that night coming in by boat in a gale of twenty-foot waves and, as I expected, they were absent in the morning. That plan was certainly not on for the time of the rains, and I radioed the Emir's secretary to send over the number of cots and bed linen, and make one passage in the mildest part of the weather and forget the staff until the rains finished.

But the Emir was really not amused. He came in oilskins that morning and threw them off in a stamping rage, showing his uniform patched in sweat.

'What I command, that is what I *want*!' he shouted. 'Those men will be here every day at the proper time, and they will do as I *say*. Understood?'

'What use are they when they get here? They're seasick and incapable. How can men do their work in that condition? They puke on the account sheets. Let them stay here and sleep here until the sea dies down. They're no earthly use as they are!'

'Are you challenging my authority?'

'No. But I think you'd better wear a blanket. It's cold in here.'

He began to laugh.

'Damned if I know!' he said. 'You turn a subject so artfully. I like it. Very well. Let them stay here. They are clerks. Let them do their work. If you need any help, let me know.'

He went out into a smother of rain and a screaming wind, and five steps away he had gone with his guards in a blank of grey.

And so it went on for those grey weeks, when cigarettes greened between fingers and fell apart, and a length of towelling was needed between the forearm and the accounts sheet, and a dry ballpoint was preferable to the nib and ink.

And all that time I had that bitter nag about M'aroukh. She had that office downstairs and slept on the same floor as myself but with the Emir's guards to defend her, and her retinue of servants, I had no possibility of seeing, far less of talking to her. And each day her marriage came nearer and I felt myself going mad.

What the devil is love? What is it about one woman that so excites the male brain that no other woman will do?

I think what saved me was a letter from Marta van der Hooft inviting me to Amsterdam for a weekend, and of course it was simple to fly to Paris and take KLM onward. She met me at the airport, lovely as ever, in three-inch heels which made her tower over me, and we went to the car I had ordered and on to her lovely little flat on one of the canals—I've never been able to make out which is which—and she started undressing at the door.

'I'm not going near the bathroom,' she said. 'I'm wet for you. I'll stay wet till you're in me. You like or no like?'

'I love!'

'Come then. It's the meeting of the century. For me!'

Her body went into an arc, and she throbbed, and I spurted, and again and again, I think four times, and we turned over kissmouth, but when I awoke in early morning, her side of the bed was cold. There simply cannot be a more crushing horror for a man.

Poor bastard.

She had left a note on the kitchen table, propped by a bottle sprouting dwarf tulips.

My most lovely darling, it has been so utterly what I had imagined that it cannot happen again. My wild oats are gone in memory of you. Now I shall find a husband.

He shall find in me all that I learned from you. You could
never marry me. I am at base a Dutch housewife. I want
to have babies and run a house the way I want to. Only a
Dutchman can give me that. I shall find him. I shall
always thank God I found you.

Ever,
Mart

I don't know what you say to that at eight-thirty on a
cold morning. I couldn't even make coffee. I was blinded
by tears which surprised me. What the hell was I crying
for?

For a most lovely woman.

But she was right and I knew it, even though I hated
the thought of it.

She was right.

Ah, *Christ.*

But when we don't believe, why do we call on the Lord
Christ?

Is He the end of the road, the last appeal?

16

I HAD almost finished the annual report for BB on the
red-lettered accounts sheets, when my door swung open
and I looked up.

M'aroukh.

Unbelievably.

In a white dress, with pearls around her neck, a broad
collar, and black patent shoes. Hands clasped, with a

diamond bracelet on one wrist and a watch ringed in sapphires on the other.

Exquisite.

'I am going to Paris,' she said. 'Will you come, too?'

'Of course!'

'I shall be at the Plaza-Athénée. I shall go on to London. Will you come with me?'

'Yes!'

'No! Don't come near me here. There are people watching us. Let us be near without eyes. I shall go on Thursday. I shall expect you!'

The door closed quietly, and I picked up the phone in lyric jubilation, but even when I was aboard the aircraft, I could barely believe what I thought.

But it was true, and I went into her suite and into her arms, and without words into bed, a marvellous passage of time, and her blood was upon me, lovely virgin that she was.

Under those satin sheets, she told me that she loved me but she could never marry me. I thought of Marta. M'aroukh had to marry one of her own. A foreigner would never live. I had nothing else to do except play out my time and go along. We enjoyed La Coupole more than anywhere else, and a couple of little clubs in Montparnasse. More than all we enjoyed my bedroom in my hotel, not hers, when she came in, a marvel of feminine delicacy, almost of porcelain, and I kissed her lovely breasts and her thighs, and we lapsed into a champagne siesta and awoke between seven and eight and went down to La Coupole again for marvellous shellfish platters and the joy of the atmosphere.

Why isn't everywhere like that?

Time was running out.

It was *the* most awful feeling.

I knew from the looks over her shoulder, almost unseen, that she, too, knew.

87

But I wanted her. More than anything in life, I wanted her, and her alone. What could I do?

In that darling head there was a belief. Nothing I could say or do would dislodge it. It was there, beyond any cry of love. She had been fed into some sort of computer, programmed from birth to do what she must, and that was what she would do. What she was doing with me was a purest question of her will. *She* wanted to. What I wanted was of no importance. I was the merest tool of her desire, her passion, and once exhausted, she would return to the life she knew and wanted. Ah, Mart'!

Not a man, but only a merest vital member, a companion to the delights of Paris and dishes of shellfish.

I detested the idea. But I never thought of breaking off. I always nourished the hope that perhaps she would consent to coming with me.

Hopeless, and stupidly defiant of fact.

She was the sublime product of a mental and physical discipline imposed since birth, and I should have realized that nobody and nothing would change it, certainly not the company of a pseudo-Christian, and that's all I was. Twice a year I went to the nuns' place up the road and sang a hymn or two, and that was that. And if I say 'sang' I mean I mumbled along with the part of the tune I knew. Compared with her faith, I had none. Her prayer carpet was over in the corner, and she often got out of bed to kneel there, a lovely prize to be captured when she stood in her voile nightgown and I could see her beauty. Some things about a woman are never forgotten. I remember the smell under her ears. Even then, I needed no more than that to punch the wall and curse my existence. Or the fragrance of the long black braids. So much to turn away from.

She saved me the trouble.

I came back that afternoon from a patrol along the

Faubourg to find a picture she had liked, and the receptionist told me that Madame had gone back to Bahrein, and gave me a note.

I could only take it and drag myself upstairs.

In the bedroom stripped of her belongings, I read it. The place was arid.

Darling, I love you, but I have gone. Please be kind to yourself. You were so kind to me. The day after tomorrow I am to be married. But I shall have your baby. That is my triumph. I owe it to you. Do not write. Do not attempt in any way to put your hand on me. We must stay apart. You know it as I do. I hold you in my heart.

M'aroukh

I sat down in the first chair and laughed, not a very pleasant laugh.

It was all a bad replay of Mart', and I should have seen it. But, fatheadedly, I had not.

So I sat there and laughed. It was shrieky laughter. I could hear it. I wonder why the mind certainly does not agree with the physical reaction of the body. Or is the mind superior and directs the body? I think not.

The phone rang and I picked it up.

'Jon? Listen. Khalil is in the foyer!'

M'aroukh, sounding hysterical in a whisper.

I thought well ahead.

'Where are you now?'

'Behind the Place Vendôme entrance. I have missed my limousine because of this. Help me!'

'Go through the arcade to the Rue Cambon. I'll ask the porter to have a taxi for you. I love you!'

'I love *you*. Goodbye!'

I told the porter to get a cab and, without any fuss, to find the lady coming through the arcade and see her into

89

the taxi for the airport, and I would settle with him.

The phone rang again.

'This is Khalil!'

'Ah, bravo. What brings you here?'

'I have finished a short course at Saint Cyr. I have a job to do for my father. May I come up?'

'But of course! The champagne's ready, and everything's ready except the girls. Shall I rectify that?'

'After we've had a talk.'

'Come on up!'

I phoned Tri-tro, tallest of the Folies-Bergère, rarely seen in more than a pearl G-string covering her beautiful pubes, and a top hat with ostrich feathers.

I knew she would be in bed, and that was how she sounded.

'Tri-tro, this is Jon. You have been here five days and nights. You left a nightdress here. Understand?'

'*Compris!*'

'For a very nice present, bath and dress and come to the Ritz and ask for me. *Mais gran' vitesse!*'

'I am almost there!'

The doorbell rang.

I went to open the door and Khalil in a grey suit stood there smiling, filled out, a bigger man, taking after his father.

But.

There was an air about him.

Distrust? Restraint. Rage withheld?

'Once you've got used to dealing with them, you've got to trust your instincts,' Frukey had once told me. 'They're an extremely sensitive people. And always remember they're Muslims. Entirely different from us!'

'We have something to discuss,' he said.

'But please sit down,' I said, and turned a chair. 'A glass of champagne?'

'You know I shouldn't drink it,' he said. He pulled a

couple of orange sheets out of his breast pocket and held them out. 'Would you please read these?'

They were almost hourly reports, in different hands but in excellent Arabic, by two agents, each of them following M'aroukh. I was mentioned many times, in various places, certainly at La Coupole. There were Xeroxes of bills, times in and times out at her hotel and mine, and the accounts by the chambermaids, valets, and porters.

'I don't accept this for a moment,' I said.

'My father *does* and that's why I'm here. To tell you that you are no longer welcome at Um'm Sham'ms. Your stay there is finished. You have no place. Everything you have is packed and it will be sent to London. That is what I came to say!'

'But I have *nothing* to say?'

He shook his head.

'Nothing,' he said, with the smallest smile, looking at his wristwatch. 'In a few hours, possibly three, she will be dead. Split up the belly by her future husband. You see, we do not allow our women to consult themselves or to leap barriers. We have a system of control. We carry the knife with us. Women are our love. We love them but they must be faithful. To *us*. Otherwise they die. We do not permit others to put their hands in the basket!'

'But, Khalil, for God's sake, what has this girl done?'

He stretched his legs and put his hands into his pockets.

'She was a loose bitch,' he said. 'We do not permit. It will encourage the others, and perhaps bring more respect, do you think?'

'I think it terrifying in the extreme!'

He shrugged and stood.

'Well, those are *your* morés,' he said.

The door bell tinkled, and I went to open, and there

was Tri-tro, beautiful as always, a tiny cap of red feathers on her lovely red head.

'You think I am a nuisance?' she said in her charming almost accentless English. 'But I left my nightdress here. I can possibly get it?'

'Of course. You ought to know where the bedroom is?'

'But naturally. Oh! Ho-ho?'

'The Prince Khalil, my companion, M'selle Tri-tro.'

Khalil came over, visibly taken, and kissed her hand.

'Get the nightdress and buzz,' I said. 'Would you care for some dinner tonight?'

She held up a hand.

'I am *hors de combat* for at least four days,' she said in a delicious air of secrecy. 'We have, let us say, our problems!'

'That's when *we* appreciate you most!' Khalil said.

She looked at him and blinked, blinked.

'It will cost you fifty-thousand francs, plus my choice of a ring at Van Cleef and Arpels!' she said. 'Money on the table, me in the shop, hnnn?'

Khalil nodded, manly pride aroused.

'The bargain is taken,' he said. 'Tonight?'

'Of *course* tonight! First let me get my nightdress. It was a waste bringing it. Five nights naked. Why did I trouble?'

She skipped into the bedroom, and Khalil looked into the distance.

I tapped the two orange pages.

'These people told lies to make money,' I said. 'I feel you should do something while you may!'

He nodded, short, and reached for the telephone.

I looked at the door, and Tri-tro followed me into the office across the landing. With two rooms between us, and the corridor and closed doors, I was able to listen only dimly, but he spoke to his father and somebody else for nearly thirty minutes. I played girl-games on her lovely long legs, and she was more than willing. Khalil almost caught us, and Tri-tro went in front of me so that I, as they say in other places, might adjust my dress. She had no need.

'Well, that's over,' Khalil said in a wide smile. 'M'aroukh is perfectly safe. She'll be married tomorrow. Where can we get white roses?'

'Downstairs at the florist. Where else?'

He picked up the phone and ordered twenty dozen white roses, and a 747 to take them to her.

Tri-tro's eyes really did sparkle with appreciation.

'You oil boys certainly have a way!' she said, and crossed her knees so that Khalil could see all the way, and that he was charmed was obvious. 'Where do we meet tonight, and when?'

'Ah, business,' Khalil said. 'Give me your address and a car will call for you. Or shall I?'

'You, of course. I much prefer, and bring a case of champagne. Krug, *brut*. Nothing better!'

'You two go downstairs and make your times and departures without interruption,' I said. 'Khalil, I'm delighted that everything has turned out well. Let's lunch tomorrow?'

'I think,' he said, looking at Tri-tro, 'I have a prior engagement. We shall be out in the woods!'

'That's so nice!' Tri-tro said. 'And a Dunlopillow, of course? In the woods are needles and nettles. I can't support them, as we say in France!'

'Your silken pelt will be carefully guarded,' Khalil said. 'I shall make a personal inspection!'

'I'm going to enjoy this,' Tri-tro said, and leaned to kiss me. 'Come over one night when the competition's gone and have a glass of Krug with me. I'll save a bottle!'

'What's going to happen to those agents?' I asked, looking at the orange forms.

Khalil snapped a flat hand across his throat.

There seemed nothing more to say, though while I saw Tri-tro to the door and put the cheque in the pouch of her handbag, I felt sorry for those two because they had done a good job, except that M'aroukh would have died a horrible death. That salved my conscience to some extent. Yet, not much.

But she was alive and might, please God, have our baby. That was all-important. Nothing else mattered. Though I would never see her again, and never kiss her exquisite hands, she would live in health and beauty and that was all.

Khalil and I shook hands, and he put an arm about my shoulders.

'My father said you are free to go back to Um'm Sham'ms,' he said, as if conferring a blessing. 'Nothing is changed in any way.'

'Except here!' I said, and touched my head. 'I don't like dictatorial methods. If you can destroy almost twenty years of loyal activity and work for the Emirate, that breaks my bond with you. I don't wish to go back. I regret it more than I can say. I shall see Mister Blount and find another desk. But if you ever need me, wherever I am, send me a signal. I shall be there!'

He put his arms around me.

'Dear friend, I respect you,' he whispered. 'I regret more than *I* can say that our falcons will be idle. And I shall have a long room full of men instead of your magnificent desks of ravishing women. I'm unlucky!'

'Ask your father to change it. The women are so much better than the men. Didn't you know that?'

'I suspected it.'

'Put them back. They're better!'

'I begin to believe you, y'know?'

'And promise to take care of my falcons. Abd must have charge. He knows them.'

'Come back and take charge of them yourself!'

'They're only poor lonely birds with no real friends. Don't let anything happen to them. I was able to handle them as canaries. They used to nuzzle my neck!'

'Have no fear. I love falcons, too. They shall have every care, I promise!'

The deep-toned telephone bell sounded from my desk, and we had a quick handshake, and I ran to the office and pressed the receiver button.

'Jonathan?' BB's voice, urgently.

'Sir?'

'Get a ticket on KLM for Rotterdam tonight, and begin a report for me on the spot market there. Don't stay at our place. Get a smaller one, where you'll be nearer what goes on and where you'll meet tanker captains. They're the boys in the know. And report to me nightly? All right?'

'I'm off, sir!'

And I was, because I had always wanted to see those docks in full, squalid bloom. I got a ticket from our travel bureau, and at nine o'clock that evening I was en route, with a reservation at the Kronig Hotel, where I was told most of our captains and mates stayed.

I have always been fond of Rotterdam, and all the canals and the windmills far beyond, and the *rijstaffel*, and the magnificent Dutch kitchen. But of course, the main item for me was a meeting with Mart', beautiful as ever, but with a ring on the third finger to warn, and a shy dark girl, grey eyes, obviously a sweet, beside her.

'I introduce my friend, Isolde de Wijms, and recommend her as secretary, guide, and factotum. She knows the oil business back to front, everybody in it, and where they have their offices. I leave her with you because I must go home to finish my husband's dinner. Have a delicious one together, yes?'

We both kissed Mart'—what a sweet bundle she

was!— and I called a cab for the Hotel des Indes at The Hague. In that ride I pretty well explained what we were to do and how, and by her replies I knew that she had a wonderful grasp of what was required.

Each night, after chasing about the offices of so many oil operators, I telephoned BB and heard his 'Good!' and took Isolde to dinner. On the fourth night we went to the Five Flies in Amsterdam—a not-very-appetising title for one of the world's best restaurants where, as Isolde said, the steak was like your mother's heart.

'How did you get into this business?' I asked her, over Martinis.

'My father,' she said. 'He was one of the first. I mean, of the off-shore engineers. He brought me behind him. I had my degree. I wanted a Master's. I studied. I followed where he went. He knew Rotterdam would become an oil centre because it was a port and captains could find it easily, and the banks were there, *and* the agents.'

'What did you do to help?'

'You ask for secrets?'

'No. Just what did you do?'

'Simple. I was the little one who went in when the price was going down, and I bought. When the big ones made two and three hundred thousand a day, so did I in my small way!'

'You must have made a lot of money?'

'Naturally. These people generally have no clear idea of what they are doing. It's a nervous market. They never know what they are going to be offered. Some of the big ones pretend. They are soon found out.'

'If you had real capital?'

She lifted the beautiful grey eyes so solemnly.

'It is my dream,' she said, over a plate of braised whiting. 'Of course, they would never consider that a girl could be a serious competitor. I would teach them!'

'All right. You've got it!'

'How much?'

'Half a million dollars?'

'A million would be better.'

'Why?'

'I could buy so much more. Where I want to buy, and I could pay out little commissions to those wishing to help me.'

'Does that happen often?'

She shrugged.

'All the time. It's a rotten fabric, but men have to earn a living. You help them, they help you. Isn't it so?'

17

BB MOVED me to London to supervise the entire complex under his direction, and I found it very much the same as at Um'm Sham'ms except that it was enormously greater—so great that at first I hardly believed it. But then, gradually, I got used to it. It became obvious that Hilsly was having an increasingly hard time in Teheran. He was losing workmen in face of threats, and his senior men, most American and Australian, were leaving.

'They've had a very nice life here,' he said that night on radiophone. 'But you can't blame them. I'm afraid it's over. Get out while the getting's good. Too many louts in the streets. Call themselves students. Might's well call me one!'

'What's the source of the trouble?'

'These broadcasts from Paris. Heard them?'

'No.'

'Get hold of the tapes and listen one night. How's your Farsi?'

'Pretty good.'

'Then you won't need 'em translated. Make your blood curdle. Outright revolution. Hang the Shah, shoot the lot. Lot of people here'd do it, too, give 'em half the chance!'

'How long can you hold out?'

'Well, I've got a lot of good lads in the field force. All of them Pakis or Indians. I think they'll warn me. Apart from that, I'll simply go down to the airport and fly out. Y'know, rub out all the goodwill, they're a dirty lot. They brought us in to do something they couldn't do, and now they think they've got the secret. Well, they haven't. They don't know enough, and the way they're going, they never will. You'll never learn anything by shouting in the streets except how to get hungry. That's coming!'

'Do you think you should come back here?'

'Jon, I'll hang on to the final moment. I don't want to see a life's work go down the drain. God damn them to hell and beyond, if there *is* anywhere. No. We're in the clutch of a fanaticism that's been boiling up over the past fifty years. We can do nothing about it. It's one of the world's wealthiest countries. In our terms. They think they've got us by the balls. All right. Perhaps they have. For the time being. But a great many in the free world are working all hours to stop the rot. That's my dream. To have a genuine substitute for oil. What a glory *that's* going to be!'

BB shook his head when I told him.

'That's years off, and the worst type of wishful thinking. I don't think he's the right man on that job any more. He got lulled by good living. That's what condemned us. Accepting what comes and forgetting about the future. That's a crime. It has to be paid for. We're paying. By the way, what's your protégée doing?'

98

'Isolde? Splendidly! The way she's going, she'll pay me back with interest in under six months!'

'You can't be serious!?'

'But I am. Her great advantage is that she pays cash on the desk top. So she's always able to buy below market price. Then she goes next door and sells for four or five cents higher. Cash!'

'That was always the secret. She still goes out in the harbour?'

'On the pilot ships? All the time. Any time of the day or night. So she docks with a tanker. She has the details. She makes a buy, and a few minutes later she makes the sale. A real firecracker!'

'We could use her!'

'A few months ago, perhaps. Now she's quite a power-house on her own. I don't think we could pay her what she's making. She seems to have it tied up, wouldn't you say?'

'Doesn't anybody ever try to put her to bed?'

'Oh, of course! She carries a tape recorder. And anyway, the captain doesn't get his *pourboire*. The captain's wife gets the cassette, and in addition it's played over the harbour-master's radio. It prevents a lot of nonsense. But it's good for business. The tanker captains are all on her side, and besides, they earn more. She pays them. *Pays.* That's salesmanship!'

Isolde, in fact, was a knockout. I would never have believed she could do what she did, even with the prime help of her father and his friends. But then, friendship has its own reward, and the Dutch are notoriously loyal.

I saw her only when I took the afternoon plane to Amsterdam, and generally we went to the Five Flies, and then I took her home, but I never got beyond the glass door.

I'm not sure what happened that Thursday, but before

I realized it, we were talking about ourselves even while the waiter served the *apéritif*.

'Let's be honest,' she said. 'I know what you want. But because you lend me money I'm not going to give you myself. You'll get your money back. With interest? What about my body? You can't give that back, can you? Then did I take the money in exchange? That makes me a prostitute!'

'Ah, come on now!' I said. 'That's a ridiculous idea, for God's sake. It simply doesn't touch my way of thinking at all!'

'Analyse it a little and you'll find out. I'd like to keep a clear picture with you. I have a lover. Is that enough?'

'He's a lucky man!'

'Not a man. She is a Lesbian. So am I!'

'Lesbian? Not a sapphist?'

'Lesbian, sapphist, what does it matter? A Greek island, a poet. They matter? One or the other. We make love. In bed. *That's* what matters. There's no room in my life for any man. Do you understand?'

'Perfectly. You'll never be bothered again.'

'It was not bother. It was a compliment. If we had met ten years or more ago, it would have been different.'

'Ten years?'

'I am much older than you. I know it doesn't show, but you see, I have never been bulled by a man. Bulled. You know?'

'Not sure I do.'

'Push in, pull out. Squirt and turn over. No. I have a marvellous lover. So tender she could break my heart. There are certainly women of another type. A horrible lot. I've met them. I can't stand it. I *hate* them. As much as I hate the men who try touching and pinching. It's a disgusting world. But I know I have the best of it. Here she is!'

She got up and so did I, to meet a quite lovely woman

100

of about forty, excellently well-dressed, obviously from Paris, and with the manner of the civilised.

I could hardly imagine them in bed together.

They held hands as lovers.

Flomille, the lover, ordered a salad. I asked for a tranche of lamb, Isolde wanted only the cheese board, and we drank champagne.

A silent group, and a disappointment for the restaurant's cashier.

'Well,' Flomille said. 'I have a suggestion. We seem a little *distrait*. Let us eat this fodder and go back to my place. Then we can go to bed and he can see that we are not lying. It's the only way. It's the only *real* way for us. Do you think?'

Isolde nodded, glancing at me with a bit of devil, something I had never seen in her before. It roused me.

Coffee, liqueurs, a heavy silence. Nobody had a word.

'My darling,' Flomille said. 'Let's go!'

We got into her Daimler, and turned along a canal to her house, a lovely old place, and while they went off to do what they had to do, I was left with the drinks tray and a stroll around walls of abstract oils, modern sculpture, and good furniture.

Flomille came down in the lift and beckoned. She wore a long lilac gown and lilac slippers. Her blond hair reached to her waist, burnished and tied with a lilac ribbon.

We went upstairs, into a bedroom absolutely feminine and spacious, everything white, and I had to wonder why I chose 'feminine' to describe it. But it was. No man could have slept there without making a change of some sort, a new colour, an odd pattern.

Of course, I had no notion of what I was thinking about. Any male intrusion into that atmosphere would have been an obscenity, and after all the women were entitled to their choice and point of view. But when they

101

came in and took off their gowns almost as a ritual, I knew they were two of the loveliest women I was ever to see.

Isolde was more beautiful than I had imagined, graceful as a naiad, and Flomille reminded me of those artists who painted women because they loved them.

18

IN THE crown of Rotterdam's dawn blue, in a café along the way to my hotel, I thought about all that had happened. While I chewed a croissant hot from the bakery, with butter and blackcurrant jam, I thought of those two women in that big bed in Amsterdam, and I had to wonder, not at them but at myself. Where before I had felt roused at the thought of seeing them together, sitting at the foot of the bed, watching them caress each other, I had felt nothing except a sense of the ludicrous in seeing two beautiful white rumps rolling over and over.

In what seemed to be the middle of it, I got up and went downstairs to get my hat and coat, and a dear old girl in a white Dutch cap—the first I had seen worn—opened locks and drew bolts and let me out. I put a few coins in her hard palm and she winked, a perfect masque to a curious evening. But the evil in those eyes certainly did not escape me. Deviltry was there as it had been in Isolde's eyes a few hours before.

But why should it be evil?

Was it that I had watched them, perhaps?

Would it have been any more or less so had I watched a man and a woman, or two men?

They both enjoyed a passion denied to men. They did no harm. They enjoyed each other. They were completely self-absorbed and careless of what was thought by the onlooker and, so, honest.

Evil to him who evil thinks?

What was wrong with it?

I had to confess to myself, nothing. They were using their lives as they wanted to, without let or hindrance from anybody, and I felt that they were absolutely correct. In addition, they had no shame. Well, and why should they feel anything except what concerned them?

Light was almost up when I reached my hotel. I went in past porters using vacuums in the lobby and maids strongarming the furniture in a lovely smell of wax polish and whatever they use to freshen the air, and the receptionist gave me a cablegram.

BB died tonight. Please come immediately. MBH.

I ran, shouting for a car and the valet.

19

THINKING BACK, I suppose it took at least two months to sort out the business side after BB's death, and at least another two to find out who was to control the business. This was all legal and accountancy flummery, but in the meantime, after that first week of tears and languish when I sent all the girls home, I kept the books and the daily diary, so that nothing was lost.

A morning came, in a cold February, when Mr

Kirtenshaw, the company solicitor, sat at BB's desk to read the will.

'Because of the extraordinary extent of the holdings, it hasn't been an easy task,' he began, looking at me over gold half-moons. 'There are outright gifts of two thousand pounds to all his office staff. Five thousand pounds to chief secretaries, and ten thousand pounds to office managers and to Mrs Bailey-Hyde. You will be asked to sign the requisite cheques in the next few days. Beyond that, you inherit the entire property. There are no relatives. I shall leave you to read the will in privacy. Do you expect to retain me as your solicitor?'

'Of course. I'll need a week off to find out where I am.'

'A wise decision. I shall be ready to discuss any subject with you, as it touches the law, whenever you wish. In the meantime, my felicitations. You are a young man, but you are also one of the world's wealthiest. Cast an eye on that balance sheet. Really, a cocktail of riches, and it grows by the day!'

I still did not take it in.

It took me three weeks at The Cherish to grasp it.

In that time I walked about the garden watching the flowers grow, and the bulbs exploding into colour. I went to Holland—though I made no attempt to reach Mart', much as I wanted to—and my greenhouses bloomed and the girls planted out, and all that.

I was upside-down mentally.

I had no idea of what to do with the money, and it went up by millions every day. By the barrel.

'Money must work,' Frukey had said.

All very well, but how?

Through the Kirtenshaw office I sent cheques for one million pounds to the Salvation Army and the Church of England Preservation Fund. I asked them to convene a master mariners' meeting in London for the purpose of buying ocean liners and giant tankers lying idle, to turn all of them into cheap-fare ocean buses in which people could travel to the Americas and to Australia and New Zealand at five percent over cost, using a buffet for their meals.

I also ordered twenty of the smaller tankers refitted to give twenty masters and crews an opportunity to escape the breadlines. Two went to Tyne and Wear, and two to Belfast, to be cut into smaller cabins and dormitories, pools, cinemas and dance spaces. With the amenities of tax-free sales on everything, and without the brazen nonsense that passes for tax-free elsewhere, they meant thousands of jobs, and that is exactly what I was after.

I bought many of the closed-down steel mills, and restored to those men, too, the decency of skills and work, perfectly sure that in the stockpiling of their product I was building a measure of wealth for the future. The buyers would have to come to me. The world needs steel. We make the best. That was my faith.

Through a wonderful women's voluntary group, I put a million into child centres and battered wives' homes— poor darlings. What the hell! I sent teams of bully boys to beat the shit out of the husbands—it was only because those bastards were not thoroughly beaten up that they dared lay hands on a woman. I spent on hostels for boys and girls roaming the streets, and for aged men and women, for food, shelter, and comfort.

'You're spending a great deal of money,' Mr Kirtenshaw said, while I signed the cheques. 'Isn't that the Government's job?'

'If it is, it's not being done. I'll do it for them. I can!'

'You're not a monetarist?'

'Whatever *that* is.'

'Well, as I understand it, not using the printing presses to cover debt. Not paying with paper. With banknotes. Isn't that it?'

'Mister Kirtenshaw, when was the Bank of England founded?'

He shook his head.

'In 1694,' I said, 'two gentlemen of the City of London offered King William a million, two hundred thousand to fight his war with the French. At eight percent per annum. On one condition. That they might found the Bank of England to create money out of nothing. Remember, out of *nothing*. Read it. It's in the Charter. All other banks have been founded on that assumption. In this day, what's the use of talking about monetarism?'

Mr Kirtenshaw looked at me over the gold rims.

'Where do you get your information?' he asked.

'Reading,' I said. 'I've done a lot of reading in the past few years. It's all there if you want it. Most people don't. That's why they're taken in.'

'Taken in?'

'Of course. Only real money you can trade on the market buys real goods and services. Only real money *works*. My money, for example, and I've got plenty. I intend to do much more. I'd like your office to find out how much the East End docks will cost. The lot, waterfront, docks, warehouses stretching back to the limits of the living area. I want the *lot*!'

'But Mister Tewkes!' Mr Kirtenshaw said. 'This is surely too much!'

'Why? First of all we have to find out how much they want. If it's within my reach, we have to put together a team of architects, engineers and accountants. Let them go to work, submit reports. Let's find out how far we are from a really magnificent project. London deserves it. She's had her share of bad luck and destruction. That's not my idea. London should be the world's loveliest city. I'll do my part to make it so. Is that clear?'

'Very clear. And I also happen to love the old lady

106

myself. I'd love to see her get more than raw concrete in the most horrible shapes!'

'We'll see.'

I went back to The Cherish and the garden and greenhouses and the girls and Mrs Cawlough the cook-housekeeper, and her husband, handyman Tim. I strolled the paths and went down to the village for the papers and cigarettes like a real village squire. But I was not. I yearned for M'aroukh—I know the gut-raking meaning of that word—and within me I howled for Um'm Sham'ms and the falcons and the horses and the freedom of the desert.

Until Ellie Farquharson came down the garden, a darling slip of a girl about twelve. She was a friend of Fidelia's, which was why she was allowed in, and she came to me in the garden seat, and said her Daddy had sent her to see if I would like to ride his Arabians. There were two but nobody could stay on them and there was a village fête and would I care for a mount? But of course, and I went to the stables with her. Her father opened the doors, and I chirruped and called in Arabic, and they answered as ladies. I mounted the bay without any trouble and galloped all the way over a neighbouring park and back to the stables of Peter Farquharson, standing there with his lovely wife, Aymonne.

I knew, looking at her, that there was trouble in store for both of us. People do not often look at each other. I mean, *look*. We looked, and we knew. It is the worst situation. Was I to make a cuckold out of him? He was a big man, jowly with beef and port, and he was obviously proud and fond of her. But, far worse, she reminded me of M'aroukh. Her slimness, her black hair, her hands, and the passionburn in her eyes all reminded me of M'aroukh. That clinging eye-tingle went on through drinks with about twenty people, over dinner, and in the hall when I left. Did I feel a pressure on my fingers when we shook hands? Perhaps. But we were not looking at each other. For my part, I dared not, or I might have scooped her up and run.

The Cherish had one light on to greet me, and I locked and bolted the front door. I took the evening paper into the kitchen—the warmest room in the house from the huge coal-burning stove that retained its heat until morning—and I spread it across the white-scrubbed table and, with a Scotch and soda, settled to a comfortable read.

I was on page three when the doorbell rang, and I looked up, wondering. I went out, switched lights on, and opened the door.

Aymonne.

'You expected me?' she asked, and flirted her skirts, a twist of the thighs.

'Well, no,' I said. 'Anybody with you?'

'Should there be?'

'Well, you never know!'

'I'm by myself. I'm very hungry. For you. Where's your bedroom?'

'Up the stairs, first to the left. Sure you wouldn't care for a drink first?'

'I've had enough, thank you. And why waste time?'

'I agree. But what about your husband?'

'Drunk. Completely. As he is every night. Two bottles, three bottles of port. And then cognac. I'm sick of it!'

I shut the door, bolted, locked, and switched on the burglar alarms, and meantime she was halfway up to the first landing and looking down for me. I waved and went into the kitchen to turn off the lights, even regretting not being able to finish the paper.

When I got into the bedroom she was naked, and so utterly beautiful. A joy, replete, to look at. She walked across to the bed and got in, sitting up. I took not very long to join her, and we began at the beginning and went through the book, to my delight and to her groaning pleasure, a sound more like drawn-out sighs below the timbre of her voice than any groan.

When we dressed we went downstairs and she had a sherry. I was pouring a scotch when the doorbell rang and went on ringing.

I looked at Aymonne and she shrugged in her lovely way. I blew a kiss and ran.

Rob Winstanley stood under the light.

'I don't know how I'm going to say this,' he began, looking utterly beat, his fair hair blowing. 'Is Aymonne here?'

That was a shock.

'Come in,' I said. 'We're having a one-for-the-road. Join us?'

'Peter Farquharson's dead!' he whispered. 'Heart attack, I think. We'd all been expecting it. Wasn't any surprise. We're *terribly* worried about Aymonne. She took the greatest care of him. Just give me a couple of moments to straighten up!'

We stood in the hall and I looked at the antlers overhead while he took off his overcoat, plunged his hands through his hair, and stood, bowed, grasping the table.

'I'm ready,' he said.

I led the way into the drawing room and let him go on to meet Aymonne. He went close to her and took her hand, kissing it as a cavalier.

'Aymonne, I'd give anything not to be saying this, but it's why I came here,' he said. 'Peter was taken to the hospital about an hour ago. To the deep regret of all of us, he's dead!'

Aymonne looked at me, and her shoulders hunched. She fell to her knees, fists beating on the sofa, and wept in enormous sobbing gusts.

I poured a stiffie for Rob and gave myself a refill.

Aymonne still knelt, silent now.

'I don't know what I'm carrying on about,' she said in an ordinary voice. 'I only wish I'd been there to see it! He was a brute. I've been through it for years. If I refused him he punched me. Where it wouldn't show. I feel a relief I can't express. Should I say I'm happy he's dead? Then I shall. To hell with him. I hope he's already there!'

Rob looked at me, a wide searching look, and turned away.

'Aymonne,' he said. 'May I take you home now? Laura's waiting there. I'd like to get her home, too. She's had a rotten night. She was the nurse and general wardmaid. If you know what I mean?'

'Exactly. And I'm grateful. She's a darling girl. Let's go, shall we?'

I saw them out to his car, where Aymonne got in without a glance at me, slammed the door, and he started and wheeled out.

I went back, reset the alarms, turned off the lights, and went back to the newspaper and a fresh drink.

I knew I would never see Aymonne again.

Very well.

I find it odd that people having shared delirium only moments before could then for any reason turn away from each other.

Remorse?

Shame?

Whatever, when I called, the maid told me she had left, she thought for a cruise, the little girl had been sent back to school, and the property was for sale. It was too far from me to be of any use, and in any event, I had no wish to walk into Dead Man's Castle. Within a couple of days an Arab had bought it.

Mrs Cawlough told me that his name began with a K, and there was an Az or something on the end, and he had the beginnings of a right old beer-guts.

I had to go to London that Tuesday, and I got back on Saturday morning, in time for the village market. I loved strolling down the lanes of stalls, looking at fruits and vegetables scrubbed and piled in lovely array from the early morning. The stallholders were artists in their groupings of colour and variety, and their dress was almost mediaeval, smocks and stocking caps, and they smoked long clay pipes—little shapes in clay—stained by nicotine and burning tobacco. I never understood how a pipe was made in clay. I suppose I could have gone on in a blither like that, but I was recalled by an electrifying command.

'Jon! Dear fellow, I was looking for you. Didn't you know?'

And coming toward me, arms out, was Khalil. In surety, Mrs Cawlough was right. A beer-guts.

20

WE WENT to a pub, a comfortable place, really of the pre-Dickensian era. The coach horns hung over a magnificent collection of prints of the coaches of another time, and the coachmen's boots sat polished and enormous in glass cases, and coachmen's overcoats and capes gave some idea of the strictures of travel at that time. I loved the baby's milk bottle with a bound linen teat, and the canvas-and-sheepskin cloak for the mother, with a wonderful deep hood that came down to cover the baby.

'You have such history,' Khalil said. 'We also have history, but nothing like this. You have a history of ordinary people and what they did. We have only a woven history of princedom and a few manuscripts. They say nothing of ordinary people.'

'Don't look on *this* as a history of ordinary people,' I said. 'Ordinary people simply could not afford to travel on coaches. They used the roads, by donkey or horsecart, or on foot. Generally that. This business of coaches and hornplayers was on a level with Concorde today. Coaches stopped every thirty miles or so at an inn. While they changed horses people went inside to drink or eat. It cost money. Who had it? The poorer people didn't. It was the well-off who travelled by coach. They were the lucky ones. Just as we travel Concorde today. We're the lucky ones!'

Khalil nodded.

'Undoubtedly you are right,' he said. 'In that time we crossed the desert by camel. My father remembers many days of insufferable heat in going to Teheran, and the miracle of ice. It's not much changed today except that the caravans can take boxes of ice with them, or fly. And poor men can't afford it. I want to ask you a question.'

'What?'

'I understand you have made several large purchases in many markets. I would like to join you. I rely on your accumen!'

'With all pleasure!'

'What is your idea?'

'To rebuild inner cities throughout the country. To build homes for people at cheaper rents. My idea is *not* to make money. It is to create a basis for cheap rents that will give me perhaps two percent on my money for the next twenty-five years. Two percent on five hundred million will keep me extremely comfortable. And will allow young people to buy. *That's* my aim. Every man wants his own house, bought and paid for. I would help!'

'I like that!' Khalil said. 'How much would you want from me?'

'From one hundred million, up!'

'Simple. I deal with Crédit Suisse. There isn't a better bank, is there?'

'I don't think so. It's my bank. Isn't that enough?'

'Enough!'

'You're not allowed to drink alcohol,' I said. 'How did you get that belly. It's not like you?'

'Well, you know the Regimental Mess, and breakfast, lunch, tea and dinner? It's all the most wonderful food. And the wine comes with it. And everything else. No wonder they wear corsets. You've got to strap in the blub, greedy lot. Me, too. I'll be glad when there are no more courses to take!'

'Look, we're drinking champagne. What will you do when you get home?'

'Well, fortunately, my father likes champagne. Don't you remember? I'm sure there's plenty in the cellar. Not worried about it!'

'Let's go home and have a bottle. I'd like you to see the garden. That's one thing you can't have. Too hot!'

On the way I told him about the plan for the East End.

'It was once the home of the Hebrews,' I said. 'A very hard-working community. They even had machines for sewing shoes in their houses. The girls did all sorts of jobs to send their brothers to university. They were marvellous women. Generally their brothers became lawyers, accountants, that sort of thing. I think Hitler made the area a target because of the Hebrews living there. He flattened it. Today, it's *still* a vast spread of ruin. I want to rebuild it. Homes, flats, available to married couples and to singles. Nobody dreams of catering to the bachelors and bachelor girls. The hard-nosed real-estaters are only interested in money, never people. I have no interest in money as such, do you see?'

'What do you mean, "as such"?'

'I've got enough money. It grows by millions every day. I want to see it work. I want to rebuild, put money to work for people who haven't got any.'

'We seem to think the same. I'm with you!'

We got to The Cherish just in time for tea with the girls in the first greenhouse. All the trays and racks were coming into bloom and ready for replanting, and the colour was intoxicating. I introduced Khalil and we sat down to dripping toast, currant cakes, and Mrs Cawlough's scones with butter and her strawberry jam.

Khalil certainly made a hit with the girls. They looked at him as though there was no other man, and I heard a general sigh when he said he had to catch the night flight to Bahrein.

'I invite you all to come and visit me,' he told them. 'Your tickets and accommodation with suitable currency will be ready at any time. Simply let me know!'

'Could we all go together?' Marie asked. 'I'd feel safer!'

'You have no need to fear anything,' Khalil said. 'My father is the ruler and he is very strict. Arabian hospitality does not include attacks on the person. We are especially devoted to the care of women. And so, be certain you will be as safe as I am!'

We went back to London together and I dropped him off at Heathrow.

'I'll match any cheque of yours,' I said, when we shook hands. 'It'll be fifty-fifty. If you have any doubts, let me know. We'll be an influence, depend on it!'

'I would like an office here with you,' he said. 'It will bring me nearer to what goes on, won't it?'

'But I thought you were rejoining your father's army and running Um'm Sham'ms?'

'I am, of course. But I can always get away for weekends. Often even longer.'

I patted his shoulder.

114

'Your office will be ready for you. Are you bringing an Arabian secretary?'

He laughed, white teeth.

'How could you possibly guess?'

'I think I know you. Godspeed!'

I went back to a desk piled with paper, and Miss Moriarty was still working. The East London job—as we called it—was building up, with surveyors', architects', and actuarial reports coming in, and advice from councils and borough authorities making known a local point of view. It was developing into an exercise in red tape, and I could see plenty of trouble ahead. None of the councils had one penny to scrape against another, but they still wanted to dictate. I had three lawyers, one of them a woman, Mary Scott, and they watched the to and fro very carefully. I called Mary and asked her to dinner.

'I'd love to,' she said. 'But I've worked all day and it'd take me hours to be halfway presentable!'

'Look,' I said. 'Have a bath and slip any old thing on and we'll have dinner, just us two. How's that?'

'You're a darling. I'll be there. Half an hour?'

I don't know what girls think is presentable, but Mary Scott, when she came up virtually on the half-hour, was a real poem. I hadn't noticed before, or if I had I had passed it over, because she was part of a long table of all sorts of people, one of a crowd. It was her work and weekly reports that drew my regard, and I realized she was the brightest of the lot. Finding a diamond like that, you give it a proper setting.

'I've got a small jug of Martinis on ice, or anything you'd like,' I said. 'I hope you say Martinis. I made them myself.'

'Delighted. I hope there's wine with dinner. I need my vitamins!'

'A Montrachet suit you? The main course is a *paillard*, barely grilled.'

'Perfect. Nothing else, thank you. Not even a salad. A waste-of-time chomp!'

'Agreed. Now then, this latest report. You seem to think the councils will put barriers in our way?'

'Of course. They stand to lose their perquisites. They won't be needed. The entire job will be taken over by your people. Is there an answer to that?'

'Have you any suggestions?' I asked, pouring the drinks. 'This is very close to me. It's virtually an ambition. I think I'd kick off somewhere else if I lost it!'

'We can't allow that,' she said, and lifted the glass. 'Here's to you and all men like you. What a pity we women haven't any money!'

'There's enough of you. Why don't you go for a world drive? A pound, or five, or ten or however much you want. Create a world fund for women. Don't mess with it. Ask for *money*, for *women*. Why can't you send more girls to schools? Why aren't the scholarships available? Where do the girls get short-changed? It's up to you to find out. Put it right. With the money, you can do it!'

'How about giving us some?'

'Tell me what you want to do, and if I agree, it's yours.'

'Promise?'

'A promise is broken in the space of a breath. Give me your argument on paper, and I'll say yes or no. Here's to you!'

'To us!' she toasted. 'And every woman there is. I wonder how many'll be interested?'

'Advertise and find out. I'll give you the money. I'll find an office for you. A postal address is a necessity.'

'Won't we take money from the famine appeals?'

'One has nothing to do with the other. If people have spare cash for starving children, they may have a little more for you. Try it!'

She drank a sip.

'I didn't think you were like this,' she said. 'I had the impression you were a rough, tough oilie. At least, that's how you seemed. I'm delighted you're not. You even have ideas. Which I appreciate. There've been few enough in my time. A thoroughly bleak stretch!'

She seemed to have changed in the most pretty manner. From looking at her I would have said she had become cuddlesome. I don't know what I mean by the term, but it seemed to me that she had opened herself, lowered a barrier, whatever it was. She sat there, I thought, very much like a big kitten waiting to be scratched behind the ears, utterly unlike anything I had ever thought about her before. And what was that? Simply as a straightforward and well-practised woman solicitor-accountant, without any attempt to look at her private life. It was not my business. But with her in front of me, yes, it was. She must have been older than myself, but that meant little. Her legs were beautiful. Frukey had once said, 'It doesn't matter what you're fighting, always attack on a broad front because you'll soon find out where the soft spots are. Prosecute and keep going.'

'Another one?'

She nodded, and I poured.

'How about going to bed?' I asked.

'Excellent idea,' she said. 'It's been pretty bleak there, too! Let me finish this, and where's the trampoline?'

21

DESPITE ALL that Mary Scott and her staff could try, the security curtain of red tape effectually blocked anything we wanted to do. She stamped with rage, but there was no way round it. George Giddings, our barrister-at-law, came in on Friday night, put down his briefcase, took off his hat and coat, and looked at me and shook his head.

'You've got a hell of a job on your hands,' he said. 'The bastards on these councils are far-left or plain outright Commies. They won't allow you to put a foot in that door. They'll lose their positions and their power. If they stick together they have nothing to fear. They can block any move you make. You understand that?'

'I don't see what they think they're losing. I've got an eye on two big warehouses. Each one would make a marvellous gym for girls and boys. Completely separate. The dock basins themselves would do to provide swimming pools. The roads'd made excellent tracks. You have the makings of a wonderful sports complex there. What's wrong with it?'

'It means their jobs,' George said. 'The moment you start to build, they'll be seen for what they are. Useless!'

Mary was even more furious.

'I think you should bring in some P.R. firm and begin to write the story of this wretched business so that the public is roused. They're being cheated of enormous improvements to bring in people, to revitalise an entire area. Isn't it worth fighting for?'

'I think it is. But what's a public relations firm going to do?'

'Well, they'll go into the private lives of the people on those councils. Find out who's paying them.'

'Paying them?'

'Of course. Speculators. Land barons. People who want to see a profitable deal. There're tens of millions there. For the asking. You don't think they'll ask *you*, do you?'

'Put that in being. I'd like to stir things up!'

'Why don't you buy a newspaper?'

That was a question I'd often asked myself, but it seemed to me that there were far too many degenerate unions to achieve any sort of success. By degenerate, of course, I meant a reliance on the blackmail of more wages or a strike. The fact that the members deprived themselves of weekly wages seemed not to distract them. That they ended weeks or months later seemed not to worry them, and their losses were never calculated. But working men and women lost millions which, of course, they never got back. The unions seemed not to understand that they took in weekly dues as funds, but they had no capital. Once those funds were eaten up, they were finished, and union leaders became so many ventriloquist's dummies.

I gave no more thought to it.

Edward Hulles, our accountant, told me that the unions should have been taken on when they first challenged, because they never could have won.

I tried for television and radio stations, but there were too many politicians and the capital was firmly with them. I was not going to bid against myself.

Property and lands were my targets and I bought where I could. My architects went to build on sites intended to employ not hundreds but thousands of men and women. Still, so far I was not moving. I wanted to make sure that the workforce was or would be available, and I ordered a series of studies of skilled and unskilled labour, because work and wages attracted the mass, and that was what I wanted.

Then the reports on the councils began coming in.

I was amazed at what had been found out, by name, position and address. Most of them were crooks, but the biggest surprise was in the last portfolio.

Mary Scott had been living with George Giddings for three years and a little more.

Two men, one of them myself, and one woman?

119

Unhealthy, and in so many respects, horrible.

I called her in and she came, her beautiful self, not a hair out of place and, as it's said, cool-eyed. I waved to a chair and gave her the folio as she sat down. A pink blush came as she read, but she was back to her normal colour when she held out the folio and put it on the desk.

'If the rest of the report is on the same level, I'd tear it up!' she said. 'Now I'll tell you the *true* story. I came here at about the same time as George. I couldn't find a flat and I hadn't the time to try. George's wife found a house, but it was too big for them and they offered me the top half. Of course I jumped at it. The rent was right, the place was right, and it meant my own front door, bathroom, and kitchen. Never been happier in a very sad life. I was happier still when I met you. Now I must resign!'

'But why?'

'You mistrusted me. You thought I was living with George. His wife wouldn't put up with that. And how *could* you think or dream that I'd tolerate two of you? *That's* why I'm resigning!'

'Supposing I hadn't shown you this report? And we'd gone on. What would you have thought of me if you'd read it on the office round?'

'You intended it should go through the office?'

'I do *not*, now. I want you to call in the boss of this damn company and hit him over the head with it. Then go to George and find out what legal steps we can take to sue for libel or slander, whichever it is. But there'll be no question of paying. Make sure of it!'

She turned to shine a darling smile over her shoulder.

'I'll do that!' she said. 'And I withdraw my resignation. That all right?'

'Perfect. Dine tonight?'

'Love it. Dress up?'

'I've got a meeting with the oil overlords at five. Let's

say nine, downstairs. Just come as you are. There'll be nothing lovelier anywhere near. You know that?'

She blew a pouty kiss and shut the door.

22

I HAD never had the slightest trouble with oil ministers or their representatives beyond, of course, the usual bargaining and haggling. Things were never on a less than civilised level, meaning that nobody screamed or shouted or stamped out.

Not this time.

Frukey once told me that when he went into a conference he always sniffed the air, primarily to place where the tensions were. It never failed, and it was discernible now. They had got there before I did, and obviously they had worried out a plan that really did creak.

'Jonathan, we have worked together for many years,' Al Houdhari said, in the pleasantest manner. 'I cannot go on any longer. We are determined to go our own way, do our own business, so that everything that accrues will be ours. We shall terminate contracts, including your own, with, of course, a golden handshake.'

'It will certainly be golden in my case,' I said. 'I have a sixty-year lease, plus a little more. What do you offer?'

'Ten million dollars?'

They had all been shopping in Dunhill's, and they all smoked new straightgrain pipes, some set with gold and semi-precious stones, at anything from a thousand pounds up. Well, it was their money, and we had to pay them because we wished to fill the streets with stink-boxes, allowing overweight slobs to get from here to there without using their legs.

'The offer—and you know it—is ridiculous!'

'It's a large sum of money.'

'It's confetti. Look over the contracts. They are valid all over the world. The legal systems will prevent your silly decision. You cannot do as you please. In other countries where oil is paid for, there are rules and regulations, and contracts. They have to be kept!'

'We will defy any rules or regulations!' Al Houdhari said, on a rising note. 'In my country, your rules do not apply. You understand, or are you stupid?'

'Try your nonsense,' I said, and got up. 'Don't forget we hold all that you've earned, and if my lawyers can help it, you won't get it back!'

'Don't dare to threaten!' Al Houdhari shouted.

'I'm not threatening. I'll take every legal step possible to make you conform to the laws of Europe and the United States of America. You understand?'

He put his hands on his hips. The others said nothing and puffed their pipes. None of them knew how to smoke a pipe, a thousand poundsworth or not.

'Make a calculation,' I said. 'Sixty years at one thousand and forty million a year, or more. That's what I want, in cash. You've got it. Pay me!'

'You must be mad!'

'I was mad enough to sign the contract. I'm mad enough to fight it through the courts. I'll take a lieu on your tankers in and out. You won't sell a barrel of oil anywhere. You see?'

'We will place an embargo on all oil!'

'You can't. There are other sources, you know?'

'We shall get our governments to agree not to sell *any* oil!'

'Try!'

I went out and bumped into Bill Blades, our man in the Khargh area.

'Well, Jon, God's sakes, I was looking for you!'

'Anything serious?'

'Serious? They're going to chuck out the Shah!'

'Where d'y'get *that* idea?'

'From living there. It's the most God-awful mess I've ever seen. Gets worse every day. Our plant's been under attack a couple of times. I've lost a lot of our best men. Street mobs, and Kurds from up north. There's nothing to stop them. No law. No order. I'm surprised at the Shah. He's got an army. He doesn't use it!'

'Against his own people?'

'Are they? That old Shi'ite—and I could shorten that —called Khomeini. The original craphound. Has no idea about government or economics or anything else. He's still broadcasting from Paris. The people hang onto every word. He appeals to Islam. The faith of the Muslims, and it's very strong. We haven't got a hope in hell!'

'What's the Army doing?'

'It's incredible. Nothing. Not a damn thing. Sure, they go out and shoot a few people here and there. But it's the mobs of half a million in the streets that cause the trouble. Army? Police? They don't bother. Why should they? It's worse every day. Hilsly's having a lousy time. His plant barely turns over. Most of his men are on the streets. You can't work like that. I used to think the Iranians were decent, good guys, willing to work and anxious to learn. Not any more. They're a stinking bunch of illiterates sky-high on hash and Islam, and it's not a good mix!'

'So?'

He held out the flat of his hand.

'Just north of the middle of my palm, that's Teheran. From the coast, that's over six hundred miles. How many troops are you going to put in? How? Sea and air? Land a division or so of tanks? D'you know what it's like being in a tank in a desert? Hell on wheels! How do you supply 'em? They need rations, water, gas. How many trucks do you need? All that, with a whole nation against you? Think of Vietnam. This could get a lot worse. Bombing? What good would that do? Tens of thousands dead. And have you thought of the Russians coming in from the north? That's where the border is. It'd be all the excuse they need. Superpower, snooper-power. We can't do a damn thing. We haven't got the legs. Add to that, we're on the wrong side of the world. What's in it for us?'

I had forgotten that he was American. One can work with a man for years, and forget his nationality. Bill Blades was not a man to be overlooked, and to hear him talk like that showed me the extent of the civic trauma.

We went in the bar for a drink and a sandwich. I had given up the luncheon menu and generally stuck to a hamburger and a salad.

We went on talking shop, and I was appalled at his figures. Oilfields that had produced millions of barrels a day were down to thousands or none at all. The problem was labour and a dire shortage of engineers. The best men were gone, and the family men were almost all out. They had to think of their wives and children.

'Look, Bill,' I said. 'If things get too rough, just drop tools, get over to the airport and come back here. You'll always have a desk. There's plenty to do, you know that?'

'Ah, thanks, Jon!' he said. 'I was scared shitless of losing my job. I've got two kids to put through school, and I'm not kiddin'!'

'Go back to Iran,' I said. 'Have another look round. Assess what there is, and if you don't like it, get the hell out and report to me. Right?'

124

Not without misgivings, I put him in a car for Heath-row, shook a hard hand, and waved.

I simply did not like the idea of our seven-man team out there under hourly exposure to mob rule. I had to find places for them in Europe.

The cablegram from the Emir came in at three in the morning and decided the issue. Five pages long, it said in essence that Khalil had taken over Um'm Sham'ms and the entire enterprise, asked me to give him a London office, and that a secretariat would follow in the next few days. Well, nothing more simple. I underlined parts of the cable and went back to sleep. I was awakened a little before six by another from Mahmedin, our field office, to inform me, with regret, that Mr William Blades and his driver had been shot and killed and further instructions were requested, please.

I got out of bed in a real buzz.

Shutting my eyes tight, I called the central switchboard and sent cables to all the others to come home. Most of their wives and children were already out, but I wanted to know that they and their families were secure.

What is it about our country that makes us feel so safe? Not for us the mobs or threats. There is a certain basis of decency or civilisation—whatever that means, though we enjoy it—and thank God, it continues to dominate our lives. Iranians are a desert people with sand in their beings, and they will need ten generations to improve even to the standards of seventeenth-century Europe. I had to take note of this in a discussion with some of the returning managers.

'I don't see them having a stable government for the next ten years,' Hamboro said. 'What happens to oil in that time is deep in the chicken's guts!'

'Longer than that,' Dorsche said. 'There's nobody around today who could form a decent government. You have to look to the generation after next. This student

125

bunch we have now is hopeless. Next generation? Poisoned by this one. The one after, perhaps. But *only* perhaps. We may have found something to take the place of oil by then. Let's all pray. Every time I think about it, I could go up the wall!'

'So it's at least thirty years?' Lemster said. 'That's a pessimistic point of view, isn't it?'

Dorsche shook his head.

'Not if you've seen what I've seen,' he said. 'I think the Iranians are going to revert to a thousand years back. For the westernized middle class it'll be agony. Most of them are getting the hell out, and that leaves an enormous gap in the body politic. The best army and police officers are dead. There is no authority except the mullah. Apart from knowledge of the Koran, he's an ignorant son of a bitch. You can't direct a country with that type of turd. No brains or any knowledge. How do they deal with other countries?'

'Ambassadors?' Tilden said. 'Plenty of *them*!'

'What sort?' Mitchell asked. 'They wouldn't be accepted. Ambassadors are a rare breed, y'know?'

'The oil situation might make it imperative, and I think it necessary if only for deliveries,' Hanboro said. 'They *must* continue!'

'I think we're talking around the issue,' I said. '*Can* we or can we *not* keep the flow of oil going?'

They all looked into their various knowledge.

There was a decided shaking of heads.

'I don't think so,' Dorsche said. 'They can do what the hell they like. We can't. We're in the negative position. We can lose our lives there. Many of our best men are dead. They're being killed every day. Never heard of. Too far away. D'you think it means a damn in Teheran?'

While we discussed barrelage, the phone rang.

'I said I was not to be disturbed!'

'I'm very sorry, sir, but there's a Miss something,

126

Ahritan, I think, and she says she's Prince Khalil's secretary.'

'Send her up!' I said. 'Sorry, gentlemen, I have other business. But finish your drinks, please.'

I went out and down to my office and ran into a beautiful girl, a marvel of her type, though I'm not sure what that type is. It is tall, slender, with dark Arabian eyes that never look except under the lashes, a small, straight nose and a beautiful mouth, swollen with a crimson voluptuousness that was completely unsettling.

She held out an envelope with the Emir's crest.

'This is from His Highness,' she said. 'I am to work here.'

Her voice was full of bedrooms. But I could see Khalil sweeping her into the cushions, and that was enough to stop any notions.

'Come with me,' I said. 'I'll show you the prince's suite. Do you have other staff?'

'Five. They're downstairs. May I call them?'

'Do, please. We'll wait here.'

I pulled out a chair for her, and she sat, and I heard the soft breeze of silk when she crossed her knees. It is a lovely sound, and I'm pretty sure most women know it. There is certainly no other sound that so promotes the skirmishing of love. But not this time.

The girls came up and a more delicious lot was never seen. Khalil had surpassed himself, but after all, why do things by halves? His harem was ready when he was. An excellent idea, though one I could never copy. I had to set a standard. This was London. Um'm Sham'ms was far away. There was pain in thinking of the place and the horses and falcons and especially of all the people I had left there, but it was of no use. I could never go back. What a dismal thought that was.

Never.

I could never go back.

23

I GOT into the thoroughly healthy habit of going down to The Cherish on Friday night and coming back on Monday morning. The girls were never there since they left on Friday evening, took Saturdays and Sundays off, and returned after I had gone back to London.

But that Sunday I had a pile of paper on my desk, and I went to bed in no mood to rise and shine in the morning. I got up at eleven or so, feeling ashamed—heaven knows why, except that I had always been alive at four o'clock to fly the falcons and, God help me, I could still feel their beaks nuzzling me—and I went down to a gammon rasher breakfast, crusty bread, salt butter from Pembrokeshire, orange juice, and a Cox's pippin.

A breakfast for princes.

I resolved to stay in the peace and beauty of The Cherish from Thursday until Tuesday. I am so glad I did. All the flowers and shrubs were blooming. Lilies opened on the pond, and the birds were in splendid song. Perhaps a dawdle through Olympus might have had the same intoxicating effect. Best, I met all the girls, and more than that, I finally met Fidelia—or Delia, as she was called by the other girls, and so I called her Delia. I preferred Fidelia. It suited her. She was tall, shapeless in that pale-blue overall and the floppy cap, no makeup, just out of bed, wash, and get on with it.

Arab-style.

I liked that.

What I did not like was the way they were being treated. The food in the little canteen I found disgusting. There was a mix of leftovers, something horrible from days ago now called curry, toad-in-the-hole, and the rest of it.

'From now on, you will have charge of the menu,' I

told Fidelia. 'Fresh everything every day. What's left over can go to the orphanage or wherever, on the day. I don't want to see these so-called curries when I come here. I don't want to see meatballs made out of bread. I want to see good food. That *I* can eat! Find a new cook. Take charge. Get busy!'

I went down again on Thursday, and what a change!

What a girl!

'I had the place painted out, sir,' she said. 'It was *filthy* dirty. I had new curtains hung. I had the floor washed and stained and polished. I bought new table-cloths. Paper napkins are good enough. I got new cutlery. And I've got a splendid cook, a pensioner from the Royal Marines Officers Mess. He's an absolute marvel. It's good simple food. I was afraid we wouldn't be ready in time. I hope you'll like it!'

'I'm sure I shall.'

And I did. Steak-and-kidney pudding, sprouts and roast potatoes, syrup roll, lovely coffee from Brazil, and there were no happier girls in the country. I was happy *for* them.

'You did an excellent job, especially with that cook,' I said. 'Keep it up!'

Fidelia paused at the table.

'May I buy rose-trees, sir?' she asked. 'That entire wall's bare. Climbers in various colours would look better, and a bed of hydrangea below would be perfect. Don't you think?'

'Do it!'

In the space of a few weeks the garden changed in the most extraordinary manner. Bare spots were filled in with colour, and shrubs appeared. Fresh gravel gave the paths a rusty tone that set off the colour along the walks.

Four men were taken on to help Roberts with the rough work of digging, wheelbarrowing and weeding, so that the girls could work in the greenhouses.

I was amazed at the amount of work there is in a garden. Those girls were hard at it from eight o'clock in the morning until they left at night.

Fidelia came to my study one Friday night still in the shapeless overall and floppy cap.

'Sir, I'm sorry about this, but the seedsmen have offered us a big rise in salary,' she said. 'We love the job here, but a *lot* more money *is* a temptation!'

'One to be resisted,' I said. 'I'll double your present salaries. Why would they want you?'

'We're about the only botanists with degrees in the area. They saw the garden and the greenhouses, and we got the offer!'

'You're not going to leave me?'

'Oh, no, sir. More reason for staying, isn't it?'

'Do two things for me. Go and see Mrs Cawlough. Tell her I got the cook because it was too far from her house to have lunch and get back in time. And that I'd like her to serve tea down there at four o'clock. Sandwiches, scones, cakes, whatever. She'll be paid, of course.'

She clapped her hands.

'That'll do it!' she said, and ran in a pale-blue flurry.

Only a few minutes later I had a call from London that the Emir would like me to dine at nine o'clock. I called for a helicopter and landed in London and drove straight to the company hotel at a little after six, so that by a quarter to eight I had bathed and dressed, and looked over the files to see if I had forgotten anything. I hadn't.

The Emir came in on the dot, as always, and in evening dress, and I thanked my star I had also tied a white bow. Both BB and Frukey had warned me against falling into bad habits.

'The black-tie get-up is for bandsmen, waiters and the detritus of decent society. If you want to dine with friends or a girl in some little back-street bistro, black tie will do. At *times*. Other times, white tie is *de rigueur*. Never forget it!'

I never had.

'Well, Jonathan!' the Emir greeted me, arms out. 'How are you, my boy? Have you heard from Khalil?'

'No, Your Highness. We've had phone calls in the past month, but nothing more.'

'He will be here tonight. He will dine with us. Downstairs?'

'I'll order a table for three immediately.'

'It is already ordered for six. He brings three friends.'

'Men?'

'Women!'

His broad face creased in an almost Buddhist smile, absolutely beyond any understanding, certainly so far as I was concerned. All the Arabs I had dealt with were upright in what they did, never went back on their word, and a handclasp was as good as any written contract. I wish I could say that of all the other nationalities I had to meet.

'Jon,' he said, when we sat down. 'I give you the bad news first. You will not be able to fill your tankers any more from my part of the Gulf. The wharfage and the tanks revert to me. Now, the good news. You will have your usual quota under my control. You lose nothing except the expense of running Um'm Sham'ms. I shall use those buildings as an officers' mess and quarters. I shall pay you for them. You will take out what books and furniture you want. Most of your private possessions have been sent on. Whatever remains, please take. I may say that my officers are completely disarmed by your silver and linen. You wish it back?'

'Let it be my gift to them,' I said. 'They saved my life a couple of times.'

'Generous of you. I, also, can be generous. You will find out!'

Khalil was announced by head-to-floor Abd, and we stood. They put their arms about each other's shoulders, and Khalil knelt to kiss the Emir's hand, and stood to kiss both cheeks, and plainly there was great affection between them. Abd and I exchanged smiles.

'I have three guests,' Khalil said. 'May I bring them to you?'

The Emir held out his hands in welcome, and Khalil turned to Abd in a sharp nod, and Abd rapped on the double door and opened it, and three women came in.

But such women.

All blondes.

Khalil must have scoured the United States, Europe, and Australia. One was American, one Swedish, and one from New South Wales. They were dressed beautifully, they glittered with jewellery, and obviously they were rich men's playthings.

I forgot their names as soon as introductions were over, but almost without any sign, one took the Emir's arm, one took mine, and one almost leapt at Khalil. By the time the champagne was poured, we were all talking, though God knows what about, and the girl with me said she loved horses, which is a hell of a way of starting a conversation. But after all, it was a start, and I told her of Arabs I had ridden and the breeding, such a strict part of Arabian horsemanship.

'We didn't exactly breed,' she said. 'We brought in a stallion a couple of times a year, and we got the mounts we had to have for the farm. I loved to watch those mares getting banged. I tried to feel it was me. I was only a schoolgirl but I knew the facts. We had a place north of Melbourne. I used to stay there with an aunt to go to school, and go home weekends. But my dad was a dead drunk, so it was no pleasure. He was after me. My mum was real wore out, and things never went very well. She was a Russki. Never got the hang of English. But she

132

taught me Russian, and when I left school, I got a job with a press organization, and I translated Russian better than anybody else, so they sent me to Beirut. That's when life began for me. Restaurants and night clubs every night. Arabs, 'course. They had the money, and I started to make a lot. Then one of them said, "Listen, I'll set you up in Paris. How about it?" So I said, "Sure", and off I went to Paris. He was only there once a month, but he sent his friends. Fine with me. They chucked money around, I mean, the way you'd never believe it. The entire chorus line at the Crazy Horse, ten thousand francs each whenever he went in. 'Course they gave him a show whenever he wanted it, and my word, what a show! I learned a lot. The right way to do this 'n' that. If you don't see, you can't learn, can you?'

'True enough!'

The table was alive with a clatter of cutlery and talk, and a string band played downstairs.

'How d'you like London?' I asked.

'Love it,' she said. 'Reminds me of Melbourne only without the heat and a hundred times bigger. That's for me. I can make plenty and send it to the bank. Time I feel it's all over, I can go back to Melbourne, find a nice bloke, buy a farm and settle down, have a few kids, and bob's your uncle!'

'You wouldn't want to marry here?'

She shook her head, taking her time.

'Too right I wouldn't,' she said. 'Pommies aren't for me. Don't like them. Never have. A pain in the pipe. Superior. Down-the-nose bit. I'll take my own men. Least they're not in the hay with boys half the time!'

'I'm English, and I've never gone anywhere near a boy. I'm strictly for girls. Any complaints?'

'I'll stand to cheer. Look. The old man's invited us to wherever he lives. Think we should go?'

'Why not? Nothing'll happen there that doesn't

133

happen here. You'll be perfectly safe, I assure you of that. And you'll pick up a lot more for the bank!'

'Natalia!' Alleyn, the American, called across the table. 'What's your favourite perfume? I just asked the Emir, and he said it's not the perfume. It's the woman who's wearing it!'

'Not a bad idea,' Natalia said. 'My favourite's Charlie. Any other suggestions?'

'Sortilège,' the Swedish girl, Bim, said. 'Sometimes I spray myself and lie naked. It's so beautiful!'

'At those times we should be near,' Khalil said. 'When you feel an attack coming on, telephone me!'

'But haven't you got lots of women of your own?'

'Yes. Plenty and beautiful. But a change of diet is also good for the health!'

'My favourite's Joy,' Alleyn said. 'I've drowned my underwear in it. *And* the bed!'

Curious choices for girls of that sort, I thought, but Khalil and his father appeared not to notice.

'It's why you smell wonderful,' the Emir said.

Alleyn rolled her eyes appreciatively.

'Maybe you'll send me a year's supply?'

'Of course. And I shall take bottles of all three back with me. For *my* women. Jon, I have further bad news. M'aroukh lost her baby. She is dead!'

I looked into space for timeless moments.

'How did she die?' I heard myself say.

'The doctors tried to save the baby. They were unsuccessful. M'aroukh died without recovering consciousness. They made a very hard try, you must understand?'

From wherever I was, Khalil seemed to be smiling.

24

I WENT to earth at The Cherish, and for the first few days I slouched about the garden kicking stones and missing meals and generally acting out a grief that seemed to chew. I remembered nothing of leaving the party. All that happened before was clear enough, but after the second bottle of champagne everything spun, and I know I was carried to the car, but that's all except that I was well and horribly sick. In my lap. Truly a disgust.

Memories of M'aroukh came to taunt. I found it difficult to think of her other than living in beauty. But in those times, clichés become coin of the realm.

My other worry was the state of my business. With Um'm Sham'ms out of reach, I had to rely on the friend-ship of the Emir, and he certainly could not have been impressed by my sottish behaviour. Islam has no place for alcohol. If the Emir and his son drank champagne, that was their prerogative, and beyond their own country, but whatever they permit themselves outside Muslim states, I have yet to see a drunken Arab.

I decided that the best I could do was to call Athens and ask Mrs Pincus back to take charge in London, so that she would have the entire company at her fingertips. That meant going to London to meet her, which was not my wish, but we can't always have what we want. I called the local garage for a car—I gave the village tradesmen all the work I could—and next morning at five I went to catch the early train and had a breakfastless journey. No restaurant car. I don't know what's happened to British trains. Once we were the world's best, but now we are pretty well a laughing-stock. On an important train, not even a cup of tea?

I asked the ticket-collector, and he smiled.

'No staff, sir!' he said. 'If we had 'em we couldn't pay 'em. Simple as that!'

There was something of a tocsin about it. A once-great country unable to afford a wage bill that would allow a traveller to buy a cup of tea?

For God's sake.

I went into the coffee room at the hotel and had a rolls-and-coffee breakfast, not what I wanted either, but Mrs Pincus was due and I met her in the office, sunburnt to the peeling stage and looking slim, lovely, alive for the job. The paper—and there was a lot of it—took no time because she knew it all by heart, but she was a little worried about Um'm Sham'ms, and I told her what had happened.

'That lovely girl, dead?' she whispered. 'Ah, no. It simply isn't right. They don't take enough care of their women. I've seen what goes in their hospitals. It's a horror. I was appalled. Poor girl. Just butchered and shoved in the desert. Muslim-style. To hell with it! I prefer the Christian, though I'm not one. I don't believe *any*thing. I like going to cathedrals, especially the Greek and Russian. I love the music and the choirs. If anything'd make me believe, it's that. But if you look round, it's ridiculous to believe in a loving God. The people most wanting help don't get it. How about the Africans? Takes world charity. Even then it's not enough. Is it?'

'If you had money, what would you do?'

She looked away, twirling a red pencil.

'Don't know,' she said. 'Whole thing's too big. It's not just West Africa, East Africa, it's all over. And then there's Europe. Have a look at Greece. The poverty's terrible. Look at our own country. What're you going to do? Almost two million out of work. What'll happen?'

'I believe the most anybody can say is, God knows and He won't tell. I believe all the so-called economists are a bunch of nuts. No two agree. I don't believe the answer's in decimals or statistics. The answer's in what you can put in the kitty to create jobs. Without the kitty there *aren't* any jobs. Work it out from there!'

'I don't see what you're getting at,' she said.

'How did the Industrial Revolution start? Two or three men made the first inventions. The lads with the money followed on. The money made the machine go. The machine started making money. A financial world was created. The machine went on making money and don't forget it was gold. Sovereigns. The Bank of England went on issuing banknotes promising to pay the value printed, and a wad of paper was more comfortable to carry than a pocket heavy with cold coins. So we've had printing-press money since the early eighteenth century. What happened to give it a bad name?'

'Too much was printed?'

'It's all we've ever used in smaller transactions. But the more important ones are handled by cheque. It'd be most interesting to know how much money passes from the presses in a year, and how much debt is satisfied by cheque. We're going over two million unemployed. Each of them has a take-home pay from unemployment insurance. If it's an average of fifty pounds a week, that's fifty times two million, let's say. That's more or less one hundred million a week. In printed money. Multiply that by fifty-two and you get a yearly payout of almost a billion-and-half of printed money. Of course it helps to shore up the domestic economy. Without it, people might starve. But while the monetarists are trying to close one hole down here, they're opening a larger one up there. And an unemployed work force is in a simmer that could break into open rebellion. It shouldn't be discounted. We're British people and we know when enough is enough. I believe the limit has almost been reached. What do you say to that?'

'I'm floundering,' Mrs Pincus said, so very sadly. 'I came out top of my accountancy course. That's why BB took me on. But they never taught us anything about this. I never knew the Bank of England began that early, for a starter. I thought it was more recent. Y'know, well, sort-of Victorian. But where *does* the money come from? I could never trace it back!'

'Well, it's partly credit, and you use cheques. Or else it's cash and you use the notes. In between, there's a hell of a lot of sleight-of-hand. The bankers and stock-brokers are past masters at making something look like nothing, and that's why they can't be caught. Or haven't been. Their day is coming to an end!'

'How?'

'Well, now we're getting into the land of daydreams. If I had any authority, I'd clean out Wormwood Scrubs, put the inmates in a military camp or send a lot of them home. Those inside are mostly unlucky anyway. Then I'd send squads of police around in early-morning raids and round up the top bankers, stockbrokers, currency operators, jobbers, and trade union leaders, and I'd have the mess tables covered with green baize, and I'd sit them all down, and I'd tell them that they were to summarize a national plan to get the country going. I'd also have the nabobs of the industrial world there, and the heads of the nationalized industries. The sooner they agreed, the sooner they'd go home. We'd try the plan for two years, and if it showed signs of working, very well. But if not, they'd be back. How's that strike you?'

'Marvellous!' she said. 'If they can't do it with *their* brains, who can?'

I lit a cigarette for her, and one for me.

'Exactly,' I said. 'Who?'

'Doing anything tonight?' she asked, picking up her handbag and a sheaf of documents. 'I've been a holy sister for too long!'

138

'No action in Athens or Piraeus?'

'No *what*? You know Greeks! It was a battle night after night. But when I'm the boss I have to act like one. My girls wouldn't have respected me. BB always said, "Be careful to retain the respect of your staff. Lose that, you've lost the lot." He was right, as he always was. So? I've been careful. And it doesn't suit me. I'm room 118. After dinner? About ten?'

'I'll be there!'

I sent a kiss to the closing door.

Ten o'clock seemed a long way off, but the space sharpened appetite and that was fine with me.

25

I HAD long worked a regular schedule at the office, which laid down that from 9 a.m. we worked on all the outside interests till one o'clock and luncheon, and from 3 p.m. to six on the oil business. In that way nothing got mixed and I was always abreast or ahead of what went on.

But on a Wednesday morning Hilsly came in, looking more like his old self.

'Won't take your time,' he said. 'Got something might interest you. Know a girl in Rotterdam called Isolde de Wijms?'

'Quite well. Yes?'

'I'm afraid she's being really naughty. Probably always was. For proof you'd have to put a couple of inspectors on it. It's tricky!'

'Well, what is it?'

'You know that tankers go missing?'

'Too many!'

'That's right. They take on a load, and then they're

never seen again. But if you follow it down, that load's sold in some port or other, and the ship's scuttled. Isolde gets cash for the oil and splits it with the captain, and he pays the crew to keep their mouths shut. No panic. Just a nice piece of business. Nobody's hurt except the insurance wallahs. They haven't got a leg to stand on. They pay up. Isolde takes it in twice. Nice?'

'You're talking about millions!'

'True!'

'Where do I come in?'

'You've got a bran-spanking-new super-tanker. It's been rented to the Eaves-May Oil Company, Limited. That's Isolde de Wijms. All *you* have to do is start sticking your nose in. You'll soon find out. And the insurers'll love you!'

'Where did you get this from? I thought you were finished with oil?'

'A very old friend of mine, just back from the Gulf. Apparently everybody's talking about it, but nothing's being said openly because there's a law of slander!'

I called Collingwoods, the Lloyd's investigators, and they put a couple of men on Isolde and the Eaves-May concern, and I told Mrs Pincus to ask our laywers to inform her that the contract about to be written would not be confirmed, and that any business between us was at an end.

'That should do it,' Hilsly said. 'She's a tough bit. She's got a wealthy partner. Owns the best brothels in The Hague, Rotterdam and Amsterdam. Matter of millions.'

'Then why did she come to me for a loan?'

'Come *on*. She didn't have to pay interest, did she? She gets enough to put herself in the running, she pays you off, and her partner provides the rest. And she can. They're a smart team!'

I thought of glistening pink tongues fluttering in

pubic hair, white rumps in a roll, and moans, sounds of the coven.

It stuck in the strangest way. After all, if we could amuse ourselves, why not women? I felt impoverished that I had never known that sort of fun with a woman. At least, I was educated to know that women, or some of them, had a more beautiful idea of pleasure than many of us, the bulls, the pushers-in, squirt, and turn over to sleep.

'There's something else,' Hilsly said. 'I'm told that the Emir isn't terribly pleased with you!'

'For God's sake why?'

'Burdock, the chap I met? He said the air was extremely sticky when your name was mentioned. He doesn't think you'll do much business there. Any idea why?'

'Not that I can think of.'

Hilsly finished his drink and got up.

'I think that's about all I came to say,' he said. 'There are danglers, of course, but you'll have to grab them. I'm not in the business any more. My factories are almost ready. Want a piece more?'

'How much?'

'A million'll do it nicely. I'll be in touch about the shares. Why not come down to the factory?'

'With pleasure. Let me know.'

But at nearly half-past three, the door flew open, and there was Isolde, with Miss Moriarty behind her trying to stop her.

Isolde, still as beautiful, in black, with a little hat of black velours.

'Why are you doing this?' she screamed. 'Trying to ruin me!'

'Ernestine, call the guards. Take her out!'

Isolde screamed again.

'No!' she breathed, into her hands. 'I wanted to say, I

can make my pile with this deal and get out of the game. I don't want any more of it. Please, *please* sign the contract for the *Sundral*. You can have anything you like!'

She lifted her skirts over the garter line.

I nodded to Ernestine, and the guards came in.

'What you have to offer is old stuff,' I said. 'Go back and face what's waiting for you in Rotterdam. Here, a cunt is not enough. You made a mistake!'

The guards had to pick her up, kicking. She had no panties on. She had come prepared. I thanked Mrs Pincus. Because of her, I was wrinkled, flat, and not in the least tempted.

Later on, of course, I might have thought better. She *was* a lovely girl. But thinking of that white bedroom in Amsterdam, I wondered.

I took a pile of documents and went to The Cherish for a longer weekend than usual, and I was more than half-way through when I got a call on the radio-link that the Emir and Khalil would be in the office on Monday, and they wanted to see me at eleven o'clock. I told Mrs Pincus to find out where they were staying and to apologise that I would find it difficult to reach London before three. Then I chose a stick and went for a stroll in the garden, and it *was* a garden, everywhere a massing of colour, and I began to realize what Frukey had left me. It was a place of peaceful retreat, and so he must have found it. The girls had put a seal of their own beauty upon it. Two hours I walked along the paths, almost dizzy with scent, but I came back to the rose garden and sat by a little fountain that prattled a soporific melody, and dozed, and awoke chilled, ready for a Scotch and soda. I had a neat one instead.

Mrs Cawlough came in with the tea tray and two messages from the Emir. He expected me without fail in the office at eleven o'clock on Monday. I made no reply.

142

That 'without fail' did it. I had no night-and-day flow of oil, but I had a fleet of tankers, and I bought and sold from other fields far more than he could supply, and I had no doubt that I was worth more. That being the case, I had no reason to be chivvied by a pseudo-potentate.

I had a lovely time reading all the papers on Sunday, and Mrs Cawlough cooked a shoulder of lamb and carved me a thick slice, with her mint sauce, our own little peas and new potatoes, a wonderful bottle of Cheval Blanc, and a restrained portion of greengage tart. I was beginning to bulge. I had to watch it.

Monday was a pleasant day. I went in to see the girls, and look at the new plantings, and the lines of new roses all in their tubs, but Fidelia was down at the end of the garden, and I had to catch a train. I could have gone by helicopter, but a nice peaceful rail journey, with more newspapers and Mrs Cawlough's excellent sandwich of chopped egg and bacon with a thermos of hot coffee filled in time admirably. I got out content at Paddington and took a cab to the office.

I had never seen the Emir in such a moil 'n' broil.

'You *dare* to keep me waiting?' he demanded.

'The trains kept *me* waiting,' I said.

'You could have come by air!'

'Have you ever been through Heathrow Airport?'

'Enough!' he shouted. 'I've been waiting since eleven o'clock. It is not my custom to wait. Ask my son and the girl to come in!'

I nodded to Mrs Pincus and she went out, and after a pause, Khalil and Tri-tro came in.

I knew the game was up.

'You lied to me,' the Emir said. 'How many other lies have you told me?'

'Let's get this over,' I said. 'I have a busy day. What do you wish to say?'

143

'You are a constructive liar,' Khalil said, and his father nodded. 'You told me this girl was with you for five days. She was not. Therefore my father's agents were correct. But they are dead. So are M'aroukh and her child. By the husband's knife. We do not permit adultery. Foreigners, infidels, may not tamper with our women!'

'It is correct!' the Emir said, getting up. 'From this moment you will have nothing to do with the oil-producing countries. Everywhere you are blocked. On the spot market also, you are blocked!'

'If we were not in London, I would kill you here and now,' Khalil said, taking a magnum with a silencer from his breast pocket. 'It would be so simple. But both my father and I would be held by your police. It is not the best idea. Better that you find bodyguards. You can be shot down anywhere. Nowhere are you safe. The husband of M'aroukh has sworn to kill you. Take care of the warning. And I spit at your memory!'

'That will be all,' I said. 'You may leave. And remember, I could have had you both arrested. You carry arms. It is impermissible in this country. What I'd hoped to do was save your sister, your daughter. I failed because a whore helped you. Go!'

I went to the door and pulled Tri-tro by her sleeve.

'You whore!' I said. 'You dirty whore!'

She laughed and pulled the sable coat closer, rubbing her thumb against her forefinger.

'Money!' she said. 'What is better than money?'

'I hope you were well paid?'

'Ho! But the gentlemen were marvellously generous, and so kind. I am going to stay with them.'

'I wish you nothing but the whore's blight, with ever-lasting buboes!'

'Come!' the Emir said. 'Let us leave this dog in his kennel. He has not much time!'

144

'May he flame in hell!' Khalil said, and he followed Tri-tro out. Mrs Pincus prevented his slamming the door.

'Well,' she said. 'That's a nice lot, I must say!'

'I think you'd better call a security company and have a twenty-four-hour guard on the floor below. I'm not sure about The Cherish. I'll ask the local police to sharpen their watch. I think that ought to do it?'

'You're taking it seriously?'

'We've had Arabs killed on the streets. The other day one was shot dead on his own doorstep. Of course I take it *very* seriously. Arabs say what they mean!'

'I'll get on to that security job. Have them up here tonight. D'you think the girls are in danger?'

'None. Arabs don't fight women. They murder their own, for one reason or another. But they don't fight the sex. Men, yes!'

26

THURSDAY AFTERNOON I went with Hilsly down to Hariston Manor. I was amazed at the size of the place. His architects had transformed an old manor house into a front for three long buildings stretching behind, and six hundred girls in trainee clothing studied to make the many models to be sold. They were all in pink or pale blue or light green or marine blue, with head scarfs of the same colour. I watched their hands, amazed at the gentle dexterity, and I was so absorbed I hardly had time to move out of the way of the tea and coffee trolley.

'Tea and coffee are always on tap,' Hilsly said. 'Makes

a nice break, and a girl can work with a cup at her elbow, in a holder. We find it's a time-saver. The buses call for them in the morning and if they've got babies or toddlers, there's a crêche and a big kindergarten, so that's one worry off their minds. They get free medical care, there's a pension fund, and they're paid full time when they're having a baby. Approve?'

'Wholeheartedly!'

'Good. A lot of people say we're doing too much for them.'

'Find out who they are and buy their shares for me. From what I've seen, you're going to do very well.'

We walked the length of those long rows of girls and turned into a corridor with two armed guards at the entry, and Hilsly nodded me in.

'Taking no chances,' he said. 'Secrets are secrets. Inside here we've got the computer of all computers. It's been in the building stage since before I took over the company. Now it's finished, I'm afraid of it!'

He pressed a button, and a panel light flashed.

'Names?' an automatic voice said.

'Hilsly and Tewkes.'

'Pass.'

The door slid, and we went into a small room, riveted in steel, with a door opposite. Again a panel flashed.

'Show identity,' the voice said.

Hilsly held up a plastic card.

'I vouch for my companion,' he said.

'Pass.'

'Is this the security nonsense of the future?' I asked.

''Fraid so. There's so much industrial stealing and spying that this really is the only way of doing things. We're suspicious of everybody. Everything. With that activity outside there, and this in here, we could lose an investment of more than seven million quid. It's not my idea. So we keep things hidden. Agree?'

'Of course. Any idea who the "enquirers" are?'

'For the moment, no. Could be Russians. No proof. Could be Americans. Again, no proof.'

'Americans?'

'Why not. They're very much in this business, aren't they? They know about this, or they have an idea where we're going. Educated young men, handsome, with that attractive accent, they'll break down any woman's wall. Especially these girls. Outer suburbanites. They seem to be easy pickings for the sort recruited by the various agencies. I said, *seem* to be. But our girls've all been warned about handsome lads wanting to pick them up. They've all been told that if they're asked for a date, to accept. After all, it's free. They come to the office and take out a recorder the size of a pocket watch, very thin, and at the same time the conversation is recorded, it's transmitted to the central data bank, here!'

'Suppose there are dozens?'

'No problem. You'd be surprised how many have been winkled out. And the girls get a nice cash reward. They love it!'

'Any slip-ups?'

'None. These girls are absolutely loyal. And besides, they like their jobs. D'you ever have any trouble?'

'So far, not.'

But I began to worry. I had sixteen factories producing items supposed to be secret, and I wondered what the security systems were, or if there were any that needed a jolt.

I told Mrs Pincus to call our security company and arrange for break-ins at all of them in the next few days. Those break-ins were all successful, and a variety of stolen items on my desk were proof.

I asked Hilsly to turn his team onto all my plants, and within the week we were as safe as we ever would be. But I was not satisfied. I had ample evidence that I was being attacked, so far without a merest whisper of the identity of the attackers.

'Best idea is to find out who'd be most likely to profit,' George Giddings said. 'If we can put a finger on them, that's it. I'll do the rest. Who's your greatest rival?'

'Hanged if I know. I didn't think I had any. My businesses are so far from the ordinary market that rivals come up in the mist. I can't even name one. I've seen nothing to show me I *have* any. Sounds ridiculous, doesn't it?'

As ever, Mrs Pincus put her finger on the man and the company he represented. It was fifty percent mine, and the rest were Arab princes. It was a shock. The Emir's threat seemed to be working.

'His name is Ammaus Rerong Dzi, and he was once employed by this company,' she said. 'You may remember him. He knows the game very well. He simply follows what you buy. He also has a working relationship with the lady in Rotterdam. Surprise?'

'Birds of a feather?'

'Let's say, just birds?'

'How do you know about them?'

'They've been trying to take our secretaries away from us. We know all about them. They offer a thousand a week for five years. Most girls can't resist it. All they've got to do is open their mouths and legs!'

'I haven't noticed any big turnover in our staff?'

'You won't. We *like* what *we* like, and we *don't* like what we *don't* like!'

'D'you think I should put up their salaries?'

'That'd be a big help. Double their money and you'll have the best staff there is in this world!'

'Double it. All round.'

'We'll never be bothered again. Now, this man Dzi. I believe we can lead him right up the garden. And put his head in the sump!'

148

'Leave it to me. I know what to do!'

I called in Captain Svend Olafsson, my senior officer, and mentioned the scuttlings.

'We don't talk about much else, sir,' he said, stone-faced. 'You will see that the masters and mates of those ships are without certificates? From our point of view, comedians!'

'Then, great God, how do they get crews?'

'There's a man on the bridge, and they've got money in their pockets and a promise of much more. They have an easy escape. What do *they* care?'

'Captain Olafsson, I shall make you commodore of my fleet. You will fly your flag in *Sundral*. You will take on a mixed cargo of agricultural machinery for Saudi Arabia with several other small items, and you will pick up a cargo of oil from a place to be named. But you and your officers will be ordinary seamen. Your crew will be masters and mates of your own choosing. All of them registered!'

His eyes glinted a smile, and it *was* a glint, and the eyes were ice-blue.

'You will take the oil wherever you are told by the captain appointed to command. You will obey his orders until you reach the port of discharge. It could be anywhere. On the outward voyage you will all be offered sums. Very large sums. You will accept. You will fall in with whatever instructions you are given. Your radio operators will be in constant touch with this office. After the oil cargo is discharged, at some place of deep water the ship will be scuttled. You will prevent that, and you will take command. Put the so-called officers in irons and sail the ship back to Liverpool. Our insurance agents will present you with twice what you have been offered, and you will all keep both sums. You agree?'

'With all my heart, sir. Every time a ship is scuttled, the complement of officers and crew are left ashore without a job. My men don't like it!'

149

'Good. Follow my plan, and when the time comes, beat them into the deck!'

'Be sure of that, sir!'

Mrs Pincus had meanwhile made a liaison with Mr Ammaus Rerong Dzi, and contracts were signed for use of the *Sundral* from Liverpool to a port in Saudi Arabia.

She sailed with a full cargo and my crew, plus seven officers, none of them with a proper certificate. The captain, a Levantine, had bought his certificate for a few dollars at an unspecified consulate.

I could see the glint in Commodore Olafsson's eyes.

I had morning and night radio messages ex-*Sundral* from the night she sailed, and the Commodore assured me he had everything under control, including the delightful news that Dzi himself was part of the super-cargo, a guest of the captain, no doubt to help in the robbery and scuttling to come. They thought.

Pity.

27

I SEEMED to do nothing except yap all day, to this one and that, until my throat was dry, and I found neat Scotch the best cure, but there were penalties. I could be drunk at three in the afternoon, and I realized it and lay down—generally on the floor—and slept for an hour or so. But that was not the way to conduct a business, and when I woke up one afternoon, Mrs Pincus looked down at me and shook her head.

'Y'doing yourself no good,' she said. 'You have to get yourself sorted out. Booze won't do it. Why not get yourself a nice wife? Away from the business? She'd take your mind off. I think that's the real problem. Too much to do, no time to do it in. So you're doing y'self in. Not much right about that!'

'All right. Where do I find the wife?'

'Plenty of lovely girls all around you. Pick one!'

'Easy to say. But it's for life. I'm not an on-and-off-er. Too serious!'

'Well, get wakened and start thinking about it!'

I did, but I got no further. The girls around me all wanted their jobs, and the odd buzz now and again on the carpet or sofa was never very much. They liked it and so did I. But it was far from being what I imagined as marriage.

What *did* I imagine?

I'm damned if I knew. I thought of going home to some beautiful girl, and having a meal and a talk about the day, and going to bed. But I could have that now. Any night of the week.

But there was a snag.

As things were, there was nothing to stop us both going to bed on the night after with somebody else.

No.

She had to be mine, and mine alone.

But who the hell was I to lay down conditions? Did I obey?

It was a thought I took with me down to The Cherish, although there was little use in thinking about it. A couple of hours in the peace of the garden gave me some mental rest and I almost thought I heard Frukey's voice saying, 'Don't worry, son, as long as you are doing good work and helping people, the Lord God will take care of you, like it or not.'

I think that was the first time I had ever thought about God. I had certainly never heard Frukey talk about religion or anything to do with it except for the help he gave the nuns up the road. I wondered how they were

151

getting on without me. I went in the house to telephone our switchboard and asked them to find the Mother Superior, and—coincidence or not—through the door panels I saw Fr Terence Poole smiling at me.

'I'm glad to find you in,' he said.

'Welcome. Please sit down. I was just ringing the convent in the Gulf to find out what's been happening since I left. It's not a quiet place. I should have asked before, but kindness slips our minds.'

'About that very thing I came to see you,' he said. 'I'll make it bald and plain. Relying on your kindness. The roof of my church needs repair. No use thinking about local help. It would take years. They'll put pennies in the bag. What I need is thousands, and it's a dream. I know that income tax is a terrible problem, but could you possibly find it in the kindness of your heart to give me enough at least to stop the rain from staining my altar?'

The small voice and the appeal of a good man affected me in a subtle way. If he with his prayers could not find the answer to his plight, why come to me? Well, bloody fool, because he was led and his prayers were answered.

'Is anything else needed?'

He laughed, clasping his hands, looking up.

'The stone needs repointing. There's rot in the timbers. Shall I make a catalogue?'

'No, but you can give me an architect's report, with an estimate. I'll foot the bill. But don't leave anything out. Let's have a new church while we're about it. Start *now*!'

The telephone rang.

'Yes?'

'Mister Tewkes?'

'You're the Mother Superior at the convent. I know your voice.'

'Absolutely right!'

'What's been happening? Anything you want?'

'Oh, *so* many things. Medicines. Surgical supplies.

Drugs. Everything's in desperately short supply. And the battle seems to be coming nearer!'

'Doesn't the Emir help you?'

'Poor man. He's badly in need of help himself. His casualties are awful. They'll wear him down. From what I see here, I don't think he'll last very long!'

'Ah. Aha. What will you do if the day comes?'

'Pray.'

'I'll send a plane for you immediately!'

'We have more than four hundred casualties here. What's the use of a plane? We could never leave, could we?'

I could hear the darling woman's voice and I saw her long white skirts.

'What do you suggest I do?'

'Send us what you can. As soon as possible, and food for the children. We haven't enough. And the newborn are dying. I'm horrified I became a nun because we have no milk for them to suckle!'

'A flight will be on its way with all you asked for,' I said. 'More flights to follow. A special flight will pick you up at Bahrein whenever needed. You will give the command.'

'Command? I? How could I, with all these patients to take care of?'

'Father Poole is here with me. He will give you a little prayer. Will you join with him?'

Fr Poole was on his knees and crying as a small boy. He knew the straits of want.

He took a worn leather book from an inner pocket of his cassock and moved the ribbon and began to read in Latin, the noble language that I had always wanted to learn and never had. Why the sound of Latin confers such a sense of truth and beauty is beyond me, but the fact is that prayer seems to wake up when Latin is spoken. It becomes merely pudgy in English, of little

153

value and of even smaller sense. I begin to believe that we grope in prayer, though I never consciously prayed. I knew from the nuns down the road at Um'm Sham'ms, that prayer has an enormous value and in their submission, it worked. I saw it.

Listening to the Latin, I could smell incense, the most powerful appeal to the human mind, taking it from the ridiculous level of camphor in Sunday clothing to the strange beauty of a different world. The world of loveliness we all want and need.

Fr Poole intoned 'Amen' and crossed himself, and so, for some reason, did I. He saw it and smiled.

'I believe I have a lapsed Catholic on my hands,' he said, still in that smile. 'The very prey I'm licensed to hunt for. I hope you'll let me visit you again? Or why not come to the church you're going to rebuild?'

'If I do, you'll say no word of my help in this or anything else. I'll simply be a villager, nothing more.'

'I shall respect your wishes. But will the bank staff?'

'What do they have to do with it?'

'Anywhere there's paper, a payment can be traced. A word to the local newspaper reporter, and the story's out with a little sweetener for the bank clerk, or whatever!'

'I'll do it through a third party. Nobody's going to know.'

'Did you ever think of a Mass for yourself?' he asked.

'I wouldn't be so forward!'

'I say a Mass for Mister Fruark every morning of the week. Shall I include you?'

'Thank you. And Mister Blount and all our colleagues. They need all the help they can get.'

'Are things getting out of hand in the oil countries?'

'Worse every day.'

'I suppose the money's what attracts?'

'What's the use of money if you're coming home in a box?'

154

'I agree. I've thought of volunteering to go out there. I might be of some help.'

'You don't speak any of the useful languages. You don't know local conditions. What use would you be?'

'An impressive block. I suppose I'll have to go on being an abject priest in a backwater?'

'What's abject about a priest?'

'I feel so useless!'

'A lot of people here would miss you.'

'Possibly. Why am I not having flowers for the altar lately, and no visits from the greenhouses?'

'Probably because of the flower show. But I'll see to it you have a dressed altar from this day, depend on it!'

He breathed deeply, or perhaps it was a sigh.

'It's the kindliness of people like yourself that buoys me,' he said. 'It sustains. Well. I'm late for tea. I'll be going.'

'Have tea here. Why not?'

'Mrs Beresford. If she makes tea, it's to be drunk. By me among others. If I'm not there, then there's an unholy catechism and talk of waste and so forth. I'll go, and save myself a further digression into the maze of philistinism and bourgeois economic rant. She's a tongue on her! But she's a good cook and a fine woman, and I've got good lodgings, so why would I complain?'

I watched him go, splayfoot, on the insides of the heels, that with a droop in the shoulders made him in a curious way look at least twenty years older, and I felt sorry for him. The thought of his alter without flowers troubled me, and I went down the path to the greenhouses and found all of them a-hum, some of the men hosing down, others sweeping, and the girls caring for the shrubs, flowers and plantings for the Chelsea show, still in tight bud but a lovely display nevertheless.

Fidelia used a trowel to put love-in-a-mist amongst foxglove of all colours, and I loved the effect.

'Yes,' she said, and smiled. 'It's always nice when you don't have to worry about money!'

'Why? Could you have spent less?'

'Lots. But we wouldn't have what we've got!'

'So? It's worth it?'

'Every penny. I'll bet we take an award. Perhaps a couple. See the village go up in a real rumpus boom!'

'They take that much interest?'

'I don't believe there's a man in the village, not to mention the women, hasn't got a bet on it!'

'I'll get Cawlough to put a little on for me. By the way, why hasn't the church been getting altar flowers lately?'

She turned her back to reach for a secateur.

'That man Bensher, you remember him, don't you?' she asked.

'Yes.'

'Well, that priest down there's not so rough, but he can be just as annoying. Arm around the shoulders, getting close to your front, sly little jokes. All that. We don't like it!'

'Put up enough blossom each Sunday and let Cawlough take them down. Meantime, I'll have a word with the traitor!'

She turned, eyebrows up, to look at me, and I saw that her eyes were the tint of pale delphinium blue. Beautiful.

'Traitor?'

'To his calling. His oath as a priest. Probably no more than the raw stuff of the confessional. But he shouldn't tempt the innocent!'

'He certainly didn't tempt me or any of the others!'

'He tried it with the other girls here?'

'With any girl. He's known for it, isn't he?'

'*I* didn't know. What a misery!'

28

I WENT to see his Bishop, not to make trouble, but it seemed to me he needed a shove to put him on the right track. The welcome was open-armed, with thanks for what I was doing for the Church, which to me was nothing. I told him about the reverend fellow's conduct toward women, and the Bishop closed his eyes and shook his head head slowly from side to side.

'I'll see to it,' he whispered, behind clasped hands. 'I'll have to give this room a good bruit of incense!'

'I didn't want to provoke recriminations, but when my staff can't enter the church to do a job, then some responsibility is on me. I hope you see that?'

'I do. And it shall be dealt with. I'm glad you came here. A healthy man in his prime has so many temptations. Not always easy to circumscribe. Prayer is sometimes lacking. Women are too often a temptation. The simplest. Eden all over again. You will have no further worry, I assure you. Was there, perhaps, anything else?'

'Nothing else. I simply wanted my girls, any girls, protected from a predator showing me one face and them quite another. Janus in the church is a devilish institution!'

'I agree. Leave it, now. Let me deal with it, will you?'

I went out to the taxi, not in the best of heart. I had stabbed the man in the back, and he without chance of defence. But I was comforted by a thought that at least I had stopped something of a rot.

Poor celibate! Of course those girls would be a temptation for any man, far more the starved, in merciless hourly desire. All the incense in creation would not and could not expunge the thought of a woman's body, naked, waiting.

I got back to The Cherish, and Mrs Cawlough with a cablegram and the tea tray. Over her superb scones I opened it to find a text from Commodore Olafsson, decoded by Miss Marriott.

Sundral now under my command. Am sailing for Liverpool. Oil tanks full. DZI and former captain went for a walk overboard with a little help. Many sharks. Arrive about 800 hours on 15th. All well. Best regards. Olafsson.

'Does that mean those two poor men were thrown in the sea?' Mrs Cawlough asked, almost in a whisper. 'What a dreadful thing!'

'Norwegian sailors are extremely rough if they find others playing rough. They make an art of playing rougher. If they find people sinking ships to make money when they know their own shipmates will lose jobs, they'll play very rough indeed. I agree!'

'Awful to think of!'

'For a change, think of the wives and children of the crews put out of work. Don't they bear a thought?'

She stood there, looking away.

'Well, I suppose like that, they're right. It's still awful to think of, though!'

'They went into it to make money with their eyes open. Now they're shut. Sharks got the bonus. Anything wrong with that?'

After she left, I thought of the priest again. Even for a fatheaded little will-you-won't-you he was condemned, but I could do as I pleased, no penalty, no digrace. Unfair. Unjust. A bruit of incense floated. But not for me. For him.

He was superior.

It hurt in a curious way.

Mrs Cawlough carried in my dinner tray of baked

158

beans, two poached eggs on spinach, a covered plate of boiled syrup pudding—my favourite food—and a pot of strong black coffee.

'The priest down the road's gone and there's somebody else in his place,' she said. 'Nobody's going to cry over him. Good riddance to bad rubbish!'

'How can you possibly say that about a priest?'

She put the dish covers on the tray.

'Better ask the women in the village,' she said, offhanded. 'I mean, you say something in the confessional and you'd find him all hands. Happened to too many. The new bloke's a Jesuit, so there won't be any nonsense after this. Same time I think we're all going down the drain. How many of us believe anything about going up to heaven any more when that sort of bloke can try tickling us up? Even little girls?'

'Try to be sorry for him. He lives in his own private hell. Before he gets there.'

'You believe there's hell, Mister Tewkes?'

'Before we were born, all this we see now was going on. How do we know something won't be going on when we die? Not here, but wherever we wake up?'

' 'S a proper frightener, that is!'

'We've been warned enough, haven't we?'

'I suppose so. But it don't seem fair, do it?'

'Why not? You have a choice.'

'You can get let down by your own feelings, though, can't you?'

'You can, indeed. That's the mischief of being alive!'

'I don't see it's fair, jus' the same.'

I looked at her, I think, for the first time, objectively, that is to say, as a woman apart from being a housekeeper, and I found her healthy-looking and attractive, about forty, never any make-up, combed-back hair, not by any means making the best of herself. I put my hands

159

on her hips and she made no move. In moments we were on the carpet and she was rising to me.

'Give me a baby!' she whispered. 'That's all I've wanted. All I ever wanted, a baby!'

She really was a beauty, and she smelled of the lavender she put in her clothes. She listed sideways, stood up, and looked at me, smiling.

'I believe I've got it pursed,' she said. 'Feels different, somehow. Till I'm sure, you can have me whenever you want. When I'm sure, that's the finish of it. I'll call him Jonathan. My ambition. My son!'

29

ZAZI LOOKED no different than when I had last seen her in her bar at Um'm Sham'ms, except that she was dressed in white linen with lace panels that could only have come from Paris. A black straw that glinted in sunlight and maroon leather cossack boots that held the scent of Hermès made up the incongruous rest.

'The Emir sent his soldiers and I was thrown out,' she said, equably, spreading her lap. 'One hour to pack and go. One *hour*? What about my kitchen property? Very simple. He gave me half a million pounds on the Kuwaiti bank. I brought my two best girls with me, and my cook. I found a couple of girls in Alex, and a couple in Rome, and a few in Paris. Of course, there are some here. I want to open a club. *Not* a disco. A quiet place with music and beautiful girls when men can come and have a drink, a bottle, with naked girls on their laps. Nothing so rejuvenates the ageing male as a naked girl. You agree?'

'I believe I do!'

'Good! I need more money for premises, decoration, wages and that sort of thing.'

'How much?'

'I don't know. Let the bill come in and I'll tell you. It will be big!'

'Perfectly all right. But I shall be first in everything. Including a real show on the night before you open?'

She waved a hand.

'It will be the best of the best. But I am disappointed!'

'Why?'

She looked toward the window.

'It seems ridiculous that a man of such experience as yourself could want a naked girl to look at. After all, you know what we've got. What's the attraction?'

'Youth, possibly,' I said. 'And beauty. There's nothing more beautiful than a naked girl. She appeals to every idiot in the mind, doesn't she?'

'You agree there are idiots in the male mind?'

'Of course,' I said. 'We all had mothers, didn't we?'

'And you wanted to put them to bed?'

'That's by no means what I said or meant. I never knew my mother. To my everlasting regret!'

'But you would if you could?'

'She would have to decide.'

She made a deprecating move with open palms.

'I don't think we're talking about the same thing,' she said. 'When shall I have the money?'

'When you pass through my secretary's office. Beyond the cheque itself, I shall not require a receipt. I don't wish to be engaged in your business. Give my share of the profit to the nearest Salvation Army chapel.'

'Then why do you support me?'

'Because we were friends at Um'm Sham'ms. Only that. And only because Mister Fruark permitted your business.'

'He started it! I sent him a girl three or four times a week!'

'You surprise me. I never saw a strange girl there?'

''Course not. There were seven side doors. Remember?'

I was learning, learning, learning. A painful process.

'So Frukey had his girls?' I said.

'Of course. How else d'you think I got that piece of ground?'

'You're simply saying we're all a lot of hypocrites?'

'Again, of course. That's how we're made. The truth all the time would be unbearable. I deal in women and cookery. Then there's the venereal aspect. I don't like to think of it. But it's there. All I can do is call doctors. Even they don't know enough.'

'Poor men. They try. But we're funny people!'

'Funny is right,' she said, getting up. 'Appetite is what's wrong. Some men are bastards. Some women are bitches. The two rarely come together. So you get darling girls fiddled about by bastards, and quiet men messed up by bitches. I've never found a way to divide them. I've never been married. I'm still a virgin. If that attracts you, you're unlucky!'

'Don't worry about it,' I said. 'Something younger's more to my taste. I'm surprised you supplied Mister Fruark but you never thought of me!'

'What are you talking about?' she said, turning around. 'You had the run of that office. D'you think everybody didn't know? You had more than your share. But *Frukey* paid. You *never* did!'

'I never *would*!'

'You're a dirty job, then! A girl lets herself, and you don't want to pay?'

'It's not to *be* paid for. It's her body. She can say yes or no. So can I!'

'I don't think I want anything to do with you,' she

162

said. 'You keep your money. I'll deal with the sharks.
Least they've got some self-respect!'

'The door's behind you. Take yourself out. You were
poisoned at that damned place!'

'Possible,' she said, opening the door. 'By the way, did
you know Khalil had been killed?'

'How do you know?'

'I had a letter from my insurance agent in Kuwait. He
says the Emir's in a terrible state. He's in bed.'

'Poor man. And poor, poor Khalil!'

30

I ALWAYS saw that pink lateen sail coming toward me,
and Khalil standing at the wheel, arms out in welcome.

That vision brought insufferable memories of
M'aroukh, as if she stood in front of me, hands clasped
in that appealing grace of hers that could still make me
go to the bottle and gulp my way out.

I had always been alone, though I can never remember
being conscious of loneliness. At the orphanage and at
Um'm Sham'ms I had no real friends until I met Khalil,
he as a prince, I as an office boy. It never seemed to
affect him, and it certainly never occurred to me that
there was any difference between us when he was on my
side of the water. On his, there was a lot of bowing and
scraping and kissing of hands. On our side there was
Frukey and—later, of course—the girls, and the delicious
snuggles between office hours. But the day I met Khalil,
an entirely new life began for me. Up before dawn to
meet him, horses saddled, splendid coffee, and off with
the dogs and falcons. At that time I was never embarras-

sed by any thought that I was living other than an ordinary life, the run of the day, though of course I was privileged beyond my knowledge.

I had found out the extent of that privilege in London. A suite at the hotel, business luncheons, theatres and suppers with partners whom—of course—I nearly always went home with, gave me a fatheaded idea of princeliness. But I was only myself.

No prince.

The odd part about all of it was that I never got a call, far less a letter or card from any of those girls. I always sent flowers and a card the next day but there was never a reply. Did they take themselves to be part of the wallpaper? Only one part to play and that, quasi-anonymously? Do the job and disappear in the pattern? I began to feel the wretched side of those lives. But if they were satisfied and persisted, then what use to worry about them?

I don't think I worried, exactly, but certainly I thought about them, and often wondered what I could do. But there was nothing to be done. They had chosen a way of life, and the best I could do was triple their fee, and once I caught the idea that's what I did, to their obvious delight.

One Friday, after a barrage of telephone calls and a solid front of Telex, Mr Takahito from our Osaka office came in and put a thick folio on my desk. He said that a consortium wanted to buy my interest plus the tankers and the real estate, all, in fact, that I owned in Japan—and it was no small business.

I left it to Mrs Pincus and her right hand, Miss Koch, a real smarty, to look at the figures and tell me what they thought.

Truth to tell, I was becoming increasingly tired of paper, business, and the nonsense of union negotiations. Never more than chibber-chobber from people with self-important ideas, it dissolved on examination. Unions have only the money their members pay, plus interest from the banks. On a strike pay-out, that lasts for a very little while. And after that?

A broken kitty and no funds.

The idiots pretending to be all-powerful really are not.

The cause of all the gloom was a meeting between my area managers and the representatives of three unions on my plants. I never took part in the bargaining, but I knew they all wanted twenty percent more or they threatened to strike. I don't like being blackmailed, and my instructions were to accept seven percent or I would shut down for three months and then talk again, but it would still be seven percent.

At a little past five, Mrs Pincus came in to say that the paper was with the actuaries, and it would pass to Lincoln's Inn for legal scrutiny, in all, perhaps a couple of weeks, and she had telephoned Osaka to tell George— his mother was English—to call on Friday week.

While she spoke there was the devil of a scuffle on the stairs, and the door burst open and a crowd of men filled the office.

'Listen you!' a big fellow said, or bellowed. 'You think because you own the bricks and mortar, you own us! But you bloody well don't. We're standing on twenty percent. You shut down and we'll all of us picket you!'

'There'll be nothing to picket,' I said. 'Nothing in or out. When I say shut down, that's what I mean. Shut *down*. Finish, in other words. I don't need you!'

'Y' can't do it!'

'Try me!'

'Y'll have bigger losses. Y'll lose the markets, won't y'?'

'I've had nothing *but* losses since I took over those plants. I've financed them to keep you people in your jobs. You don't want seven percent? All right. Go on the dole. But I won't pay a penny more. Your productivity record is dismal. You're not worth it. I don't propose to put a penny more into any of them. That's all!'

'Y' too big for y' boots,' the tall fellow said. 'Well, we'll teach y'!'

'Do what the devil you like. Now get out of my office!'

'Why don't you sit down sensible?' another man said. 'Might come out satisfactory all round?'

'Seven percent and that's all. Now go.'

My security guards in blue uniforms pushed in and fist fights began and were stopped by the older man, arms out, shouting. Then the police came in and cleared the room. It was sudden.

At one moment howls and chaos, and the next, silence.

I had time to look at myself and what I was thinking.

I had absolutely no notion. I wondered if any of it was worthwhile. I had no answer to it. None at all. Simply thinking about the whole affair made me want to lie down and sleep. This, of course, was psychiatrist territory that I had no intention of tramping through, so I said to hell with it and put it out of mind. As Frukey had once said, 'If you're in command, don't let 'em bother you.'

But there was a serious bother.

People were going to be put out of work. How were they to take care of their children? Of course, the weekly dole would help them in food and rent. The car—that ultimate toy of the half-grown grown-up—and the mortgage payment would suffer, but not the pints of beer at the club.

The creatures of the welfare state were about to be brought to a sense of reality. A harsh collision.

With bank accounts across the world earning daily interest, I was a fine one to talk.

In the middle of that, Mrs Pincus—I knew her ripple

of nails on the panel—came in and said that the Arab banking consortium were waiting downstairs, and gave me the agenda.

'I don't want to meet them,' I said. 'Ask Hassan to take my chair. He knows what I want.'

'They might vote to give the hotel construction plans to another company. The delegation from Japan've made a nice offer. You might lose it.'

'They know which is my company. You could give Hassan a hint. I want that contract to keep my men in employment. Emphasise it!'

She nodded.

'One other thing,' she said. 'I just had a call from The Cherish. Miss Fidelia. I always get her mixed up with the opera.'

'*Fidelio*?'

'Mmh. She says your Mrs Cawlough's run off with the Marine cook, and could she get somebody else?'

'Poor Cawlough!'

'Oh, not a bit. She says he's cuddling himself, glad to be shot of her. He says she was a bag, running after everybody. Now he's got a chance to divorce her and marry somebody he's always wanted.'

'Two of a kind? Routine bourgeois rottenness. Tell her to get somebody else as good as the Marine. His steak-and-kidney pudding was better than Simpson's!'

'That's where he's going!'

31

MY DESK for months had piled with reports from the Gulf States and elsewhere about conditions in Iran, food shortages, breakdowns in essential services, the lot. Nothing but trouble for the Persian people. The poison seemed to be emanating from Qum, the den of the Black Dog, as many called that little old fraz, Khomeini.

Why the French had ever allowed him to broadcast in the first place still puzzled me, although French help might—after the Shah's fall—promote rich business. There was no doubt that the Pahlevi dynasty would end, though in other times it had seemed highly unlikely. The imperial bash at Persepolis, for example, when tens of millions were spent in entertaining the world's dummies—with no more than a token ration for the poor —made plain an attitude. The poor were of no consequence and were not to be worried about.

I had stayed with Hilsly in his lovely house near the Palace in Teheran, and I had seen that opulent extravaganza of wealth and splendour, elements that my frugal life had never brought me to dream about, far less to imagine.

'Making a stick for his own back,' was Hilsly's comment. 'The people'll never forget this. That money could've put tapped water and electric light into every house in the land. As the enlightened rulers have done. But no, not likely. Blow it off on degenerates. Idlers. All the international whores and roués. People without a thought beyond their own pleasures. What do the ordinary people think? It's still an Islamic society run by the mullahs. Priests of a strict and teetotal religion. What do you suppose they thought when all that champagne and liquor was being swilled out there? That's a grievous sin. It won't be forgotten because it can't be. To the detriment of the Shah!'

'You think he's finished?'

'Beginning of the end's what some—most of us—think. This little party of his was the last straw. People saw they didn't mean much to him. So what was he to them?

168

Somebody to shift? Could be!'

'I liked the Iranians—Persians—I met. Different in a subtle way from the Arabs, I thought.'

'Subtle's right!'

Besides the paperwork, during any one week I chaired sixteen committees, each a sector of business, and all flourishing. But it was too much in its detail to keep in mind, and so I gave Mrs Pincus overall authority to design her own plan, and let me have the gist of what went on when I went to London.

'Have you had a look round downstairs lately?' she asked, out of the blue.

'No?'

'I think it's time. This is a lovely property. It's worth a lot. But the kitchen's full of rats and cockroaches, the restaurant doesn't deserve the name, and the rooms and furniture are badly run down. I don't want to lose the manager his job, but he's a drunk!'

'I'll deal with that *now*! Send the man his notice today, with three months' salary. We'll have to find another manager, though. Who?'

'We'd best consult the Swiss hotel school. They seem to have the best training courses. What we want is a man who can go for twenty-five years. And restore the place from the cockroaches up!'

'Right. Find him!'

Easier said than done.

I interviewed the few that got past Mrs Pincus, a motley crew, it might be said, though with the best credentials and an eye on what they thought the main chance. They all considered themselves ready for Manhattan or D.C., as they called Washington.

That was where the big money was, apparently. Not in a place like ours.

I dismissed them all except Guillaume Bertin, smartly dressed in a Lanvin suit and Bunting shoes, with his letters of recommendation in a fine hide briefcase, items pointing to judgment in matters of taste.

'Take charge today,' I told him. 'I'd close the hotel, but there are several life-tenants. You'll have to work around them and try not to bother them unnecessarily. I assume Mrs Pincus has told you what's needed?'

'Complete refurbishing and decoration, sir,' he said. 'I've had experience of it in two hotels in the past six years. One has to be careful not to destroy an atmosphere. I have a free hand, sir?'

'Completely. But show me what you wish to do first, won't you?'

'Sir, I may close the restaurant from tomorrow?'

'It's all yours!'

He nodded and went out, leaving me satisfied that everything was on the right course. I bundled my homework into my scuffed attaché case, thinking of Bertin's horsehide beauty, and Mrs Pincus rippled and came in.

'I had someone from the Teheran office on the phone, but we got cut off. He said that big boy had gone to America and the place was bedlam!'

'Right. Give Whitcomb a copy of the emergency plan and put him on the next flight to Alex. He'll take charge of reposting staff. Send a Telex to all our people in Iran to leave for Alex immediately. Tell Yussuf to book rooms for them. Instructions will follow. Off you go.'

32

THE BIG flap, as the office called it, was all over in four days, everybody safe in Alexandria. The outcome was that we made evacuation plans for all the staff, wherever they were, and I went to bed the happier. So, I'll bet, did everybody else. To be at the mercy of gangs of hooligans anywhere is not the happiest way to live, far less to do business. I knew that in our company, at least, people were looking over their shoulders and some were scatter-brain worried. I had all the women and children flown home and made sure the husbands were recalled soon after, leaving single men to take over. It suited them because they earned more and they could stretch their pinions, something they could never do under the senior—married, trained in the old BB and Frukey style. I was happy about it because a company needs new blood and ideas, and young men start friendships with men working for them that can last lifelong and bring magnificent support in terms of loyalty and, not least, integrity.

On a Friday night, certain that all was well, I went into retreat at the Abbey of Saint Columba, under the aegis of Brother Justinian.

The whitewashed room, table, chair, and the iron crucifix were all, and I slipped from the ease of my life in the hotel to the rigour of the acolyte, though of course I was not, basically because I had no true faith. I attended services at six in the morning and four more during the day, until I went to bed after the nightly chorale and the bell tolled for sleep. But I was no nearer what Fr Poole had wished, and possibly, prayed for, and I could find no reason to pray for myself.

I wished that I could.

What is there to pray for?

As I listened to monks reading their breviaries, a deep-toned mutter that perhaps meant something to them but nothing to me, I began to question my presence there. I still had to think of ways to get the oil to warm them and allow them to cook their food, and I did. But getting a place warm and cooking were little enough. What the hell was I doing there? Cooling the brain? Attempting to purge detail. Hoping to go back to my office as something more than a mental cripple? Because that was what I was, and there was no medicine to cure it. A different sort of life, another way to exist might be the answer. The monks were ascetic in their attitude. They never spoke to me. If I wanted anything I had to speak to the Preceptor, and he used very few words, generally Yes or No. A curious man, almost a ghost of himself. I had no real bond with him or with any of them. We were simply spirits in a vacuum of our own making. The thought frightened me, and pulled me almost as if with a bit between my teeth, while the bell pealed for the noonday meal.

I decided then, in the herb garden, that I would leave. I wanted no more of their non-acceptance of the world. The world kept them inside their walls, fed them, warmed them, men of God, merest fleas in His garment, satisfying themselves but nobody else.

The car came as the greatest pleasure, and I got in with a feeling that I was going back to a world I knew and could deal with, now more than at any time before, because I had learned at least to be myself.

Myself.

And who was that?

I remembered curiously little of myself before the time I went down the ladder from the tanker at Um'm Sham'ms, and stood before Frukey in those mud walls, and Abd showed me to my whitewashed room and told me when meals were served. There was no difference between that and the Abbey, in fact, except that I could talk to those around me, most of them women. I never realized that women were a different sex until Mrs Pincus taught me, God bless her, in the gentlest, most wonderful and punishing way. Punishing because I was shocked. That sudden and even prolonged spurt of vital fluid is always a shock both to the senses and to the physique, and that is exactly why I empathise with girls raped by brutes. They are gentler than their bastard masters, and in their gentleness, without defence.

Sergeant Mellish and Constable Lurie came in almost at tea-time, looking huge in the doorway.

'Sorry to trouble you, sir,' Sergeant Mellish said, in that lovely rural burr. 'We were on patrol 'bout 'n' hour ago, and we seen these two dark 'plected blokes swanning 'bout round here, and they turned, like, and come round again. So I took 'em down to the station and the Inspector made 'em give an account of theirselfs, and took their names and addresses. They're staying at the Dorchester and they're supposed to be princes. That's their names, sir.'

He put a slip on the desk. I knew neither of them.

'I can't help you, Sergeant,' I said. 'But I'm very grateful for your superintendence. Would you both care for a cup of tea?'

'No thanks, sir. Got to finish the patrol first. Good afternoon, sir.'

Two dark 'plected blokes? Possibly from the Gulf?

I was made to feel no better, and that was a fact.

I had a quease in the pit of my stomach. Arabs never let go, and with all the money in the world, why should they? I knew I had to set up the security guard to include The Cherish, get floodlights installed, and then find beds and meals for the men. An absolute nuisance, but there it was.

Mrs Pincus, as usual, put it all together, and the next night we had three Portakabins and the lights, everything working. Best of all, the cabins were large enough for beds and furnishings to make them comfortable, and three women from the village cooked for them in a central mess, another Portakabin. It all settled down sooner than I thought it would, and when the shotguns came in, the quease went.

We were now getting nearer to the flower show, and already the air itself seemed to electrify. The plants and flowers were bursting with promise, and the cold rooms were prepared. The girls mothered every growing thing in sight—there was no other word—sprayed water, took care, and I, the useless one, looked on, loving every moment.

'Would you like to buy a ticket for the Hunt Ball, sir?' Fidelia asked, at luncheon. 'It all goes to the Barnado Homes for children.'

'A Hunt Ball at this time of year, and for Doctor Barnardo's? I thought Hunts were their own favourite charities?'

'It's something of a local tradition, you know. *We* call it the Hunt Ball because most of the same families are on the Boards of orphanages and hospitals, and all that. It lets them trade a good cause for a bad one and we enjoy it, too, especially the dancing!'

'Buy one for all of us, then, plus fifty. Sir John came to see me some time ago, but I told him I wasn't in the least interested in fox-hunting. It's too many and a pack of dogs against one animal. Odds are against the fox. No matter what the farmers say, I don't like it! What was it that Shaw said, about the unthinkable chasing the inedible?'

'I think it was Wilde, and I can never remember it either. But I agree. Still, the Hunt Ball is one night when we can all dress up and drink champagne. I love it!'

I ordered a case of Krug halves sent to her house in the village, where her father was the local physician, a councillor, and a power in the parish.

'Thank you for the champagne,' she said a couple of mornings after. 'I went to bed slightly drunk. My father approved. He says it's up to everybody to have a holiday

174

when they can. Take off the spiderwebs of the day. It's a blight that medicine can't cure.'

Her father came to see me at the weekend, and drank a sherry with me.

'I don't want to appear worried,' he said, though I knew he was. 'There's talk going about that Arabs of one sort or another are after you. Is my daughter in any danger?'

'Absolutely not. Why do you ask?'

'Talk in the village. You know how it is.'

'Nothing but the worst sort of gossip. I wish to God they'd mind their own business!'

'But gossip's what keeps us going, isn't it? Without it, we aren't alive. I'm glad to hear there's no danger. But then, why the lights and those guard-houses?'

'A little intelligent foresight can sometimes prevent disaster. It's me they're looking for. They won't harm women. It's not in their book.'

'I'm happy I came up. No, please don't bother to see me out. My car's just here in the lane. The champagne, by the way, was greatly appreciated.'

33

ON THE morning of the Hunt Ball, Mrs Pincus came in wearing her pixie-in-ye-meadow smile, and I knew I was in for a bump.

'I'm giving two months notice!' she almost sang. 'I'm getting married. He's an accountant, too. We're going to open a business. I'm taking Miss Koch with me. I shan't have to train her. I'd suggest Miss Marriott to take my

175

place, and let her choose a deputy. She's bright enough, don't you think?'

'I do. But this is a shock. When did you decide?'

'Last night. When he asked me. I've got my son to think about. I can leave him a lot more married than I could single. And he'll come in the business. Big advantage, isn't it?'

'Of course. But even now I can feel the draught!'

She bent over me and I felt her warmth, womanly, pervading.

'We've had lovely years together,' she whispered. 'I wouldn't change my memories of them for anything on this earth. You saved me from going mad. You know that, don't you? Now the fires've gone down a bit. I can still give him all he wants. But we're not talking about girls 'n' boys, are we? He's a nice man. Nice in his way as you are. And I'm very happy!'

'God bless you. Both. You'll get a golden handshake.'

'I'll go straight to the bank!'

'Good. Going to the Hunt Ball tonight?'

'Wouldn't miss it. First one I've been to. As it happens, I've got this lovely dress from Paris. Never been worn. Bet you I'll dazzle him!'

'That's the ticket. A nice dress for a woman, that's the first thing.'

'He told me he's never worn white tie!'

'He can wear black. What's the difference?'

'They think white tie's necessary.'

'Why should it be? Outworn social nonsense. Formal occasion, possibly. But for a so-called charity ball? What the hell!'

'I'll bet *you're* going in white tie?'

'I happen to have one. And the outfit. So?'

'Be a doll and keep him company, will you? He won't feel so left out. You know?'

'All right. Most of theirs'll be hired, anyway!'

176

'Oh, bitchy!'

'And fact. When do you really want to go?'

'I've got a house to find, furniture, curtains, all that.'

'Is your desk clear?'

'Except for a couple of little things Miss Koch can handle.'

'Right. Then this is your last day!'

She put a hand flat on my cheek, and tears seemed near, but she hurried to the door and went with no look back.

It seemed like the end of an era.

But then I heard the ripple, and she came back.

'That handshake,' she said. 'Of course I'd love it. But he wouldn't. He'd think it paid for the house, wouldn't he? We'd be starting on a sour note, and that can't be right. So if you don't mind, I'd rather not take it.'

'But you said you'd put it in the bank, didn't you?'

'I'd still have to tell him, though.'

'Then I'll bank it for your son. How's that?'

'Oh, marvellous!'

'That's settled then. Leave his name and address with Miss Koch, and she'll get the papers drawn up. I'll make one stipulation. He won't be able to touch it until he's twenty-five. If he needs money for a good reason before then, I'll take your word it's correct and authorise a withdrawal. Otherwise not a penny!'

'I don't think he'll need to. I've got a bit saved up, too, y'know. But you're a real doll. And I love you. That's the last time I'll ever say that!'

She went in a high wave, and I remembered Frukey and BB, and all the girls, and it was a sad, sad moment. But there was a deskful of paper and so little time, and while I saw again those faces and felt the bodies and knew the passions, I rescheduled tankers and their ports of call, wondering where my Japanese princesses were, and if they had families. I realized that I should have

177

married and started a family long before, but there had never seemed any really good reason for it. I loved women and always had—it's not too much to say—teams of them all ready for a bright night. After all, women can make up their minds, too, and I neither threatened nor forced at any time. But there are also two sides to that. In a night or two or three, there is little time to find out if you love.

That, so far as I was concerned, was the crux of the problem.

Fondness for a girl is not love.

One can be fond of a girl for many reasons, but none of them is love. Fondness is only the bloom, and when it wears off, the marriage slips to divorce, and I was far from wanting anything like that, quite simply because I was the product of a Frukey-BB upbringing. Odd that a couple of Edwardians can affect the life of someone decades younger, but they had. I went the way they had trained me, and I never saw any other way, or thought in any other way, or did anything they would not have done. In later years, however, I had other ideas.

We had changed, certainly as a people, perhaps after Churchill lost the first post-war election. There was no more jingoism, very little flag-waving, except perhaps among children, and after Suez, no more talk of invasions, much less of re-armament. But we were still an island nation, and though we had a place in the Common Market, we still had the duty of protecting ourselves, without depending upon the Americans as we undoubtedly had for far too long. We had to find our own feet, and hold up our heads again. We had to restore the Royal Navy, bring the Regular Army up to scratch, and strengthen the Royal Air Force, but that, in a disastrous economic climate, was a lot sooner said than done.

I had ample evidence on the night of the Hunt Ball

that my ideas were not well-received or even tolerated by the bankers and stockbrokers, and City whatnots gracing the ball with their presence, accompanied by wives, grown children and possibly relatives, no expense spared. They all, for one or another reason, looked like each other, talked in the same manner, and why not since they had all been to the same schools? They distrusted strangers, especially me because I had never been to any school and spoke every language except their own. But I had money. That made a difference. I had cachet, whatever that may be, and I was treated deferentially albeit with a sense of humour as much ironical as patronizing. It takes not very much insight to plumb the type, and type it is. That night I had to sample many varieties, primarily because I was the eternal stranger, not because I was Sinbad or the Ancient Mariner, but simply because I was me. I never accepted invitations to luncheons or dinners, whether they believed me or not, because I had a deskful of paper that had to be put in the machine. I met the Iranian Ministers, but there was really nothing to be done. None of them had any authority. Any agreements were abrogated either by the Majlis or by the henchmen of Khomeini. There was no direction.

Undoubtedly the Algerians saved the day. They had enough financial inner knowledge and command of the three major languages to throw down any barriers. That was the secret.

Command of language.

That is the single issue in the entire Middle East today and for the next generation, perhaps two. How many of us—outside the diplomatic world—speak Arabic or Farsi?

The ballroom was a flaunt of colour, the lovely dresses of the women, flowers, banqueting tables glittering with crystal and silver and dozens of épergnes piled with fruit, and decorations of flowers, mostly mine, designed by the girls that morning. I felt quite proud of them. After I met Mrs Pincus and Leo McKinley, the man she was marrying, I was glad I had agreed to go in black tie. 'Nice' *was* the word for him—for both of them—and there was no need for him to feel out of place for someone else's antiquated wear-this-but-not-that. I drank a toast to their happiness, and saw them off on to the dance floor.

'Come on, Helene,' I heard him say. 'This might not be so bad at that!'

A lovely name for a most lovely woman.

And I had never known.

All I had needed to do was ask.

Still, with the chandeliers on and the band playing I settled to enjoy myself, and I did rather better than that.

Except that Sir John came and sat down opposite me.

'Hear you've been to the Middle East since we last met,' he said, in his best board-meeting style. 'How did you find things?'

'Rough.'

'That all?'

'What more do you want?'

'Well, uh, in what way?'

'Any way you wish to think.'

'Not much to go on, is it?'

'I'll try to explain. There's sixty percent unemployment. Some say more. The oilfields for the most part are out of action. They won't get their technicians back. They'll probably try to get Russians. Won't be easy. May take them two years to get back to one-third production. Perhaps more. They've done themselves a great deal of harm.'

'Oh?'

'They've made an enemy of the Americans. Never

180

mind about the offshoots among the rest of us. It may take three generations before the Americans admit the Persians into the human race. Even then, I wouldn't give you a damn for their chances. D'you know any Americans?'

'Thankfully, no!'

'Your profound loss. This war with Iraq will be heaven-sent. I don't think the Iraqis want to win it except to hold what they've already taken. The Persians were stupid enough to shoot their best soldiers. The generals. They have neither strategists nor tacticians, and in supply and ordnance, they have little or nothing. They're wading into a morass. Given the sort of idiots they are, they'll never kick free. You understand?'

'I had a few years on the General Staff. I think I do.'

'Then you were some of the damn fools who shoved us out of the oil lands, you and the fatheaded politicians. All we'd had to do was hold it. We were too utterly blind. Oil would not have been at its present price if we'd been in charge. The world economy wouldn't be in its present pitiful state if we'd had a hand on the wheel. Look at this crowd here. Dancing while Rome goes down in ash!'

He got up.

'Oh dear!' he said. 'You're rather too intense, don't you think?'

'Go and flatter yourself with that. Intensity's something you people never had. It's why you let an Empire slip out of your hands. You had no brains. The money to run everything was under your feet. You let it go. Haul down the flag. Panacea for everything. And look at it!'

'I'm glad you didn't apply to join the Hunt!'

'You invited me, remember?'

'That was another day. Extending the hand of friendship, and so forth. But one learns, doesn't one?'

'One does, indeed. And good night to you!'

I had seen what I thought was a mirage at the top of the staircase. It took me two or three seconds to recognize Fidelia, out of the pale-blue bundling and the floppy cap. She wore a long, dark blue dress with some white stitching and small diamond-and-sapphire earrings that winked when they caught the light. Her hair was a cap of deep chestnut curls, and the delphinium-blue eyes shone even at that distance.

I was enchanted. At last I had found a flower-woman.

I went up the stairs and took her hands, and they were willingly in mine.

'At last I see you!' I said. 'Out of that damn coverall!'

'It's useful,' she said, almost demure. 'I can send it to the laundry, can't I?'

'It's amazing what marvels come out of the ugliest cocoon. Would you care to dance?'

She made a wry little mouth.

'I'd love to, but it'll have to wait. I'm terribly sorry, but there it is.'

A young man came within a yard and looked at her.

'This is our dance?' he asked, but it was a statement more than a question.

She smiled at me, and they went down the stairs hand-in-hand, a bad sign. I could have booted him, but what did I expect? A girl that lovely must have slavering legions after her, and I had never made the smallest attempt. I had never even asked her to dinner.

I saw Marie wall-flowering it at the far end of the room and went through couples to invite her. Curious, how they all seemed to be shadow-boxing, pumping fists and elbows, jumping invisible ropes at some unknown gym. I felt like asking who their trainer was, and when they'd be up for the title. Others, as I passed them, slithered to and from each other, bodies hung from wire-hangers, no elbows or other joints that I could see.

Marie laughed when I held out my hand, but she, too, came onto the floor punching and slithering, and I had no chance to put an arm about her and dance the way I had been taught in Alexandria.

'What *is* this, a ballroom or a gymnasium?' I asked her. 'They all look like amateur scrappers, and bantams at that!'

That was my first mistake, and my second was when I tried the good right-arm technique, around her waist.

'That's fuddy-dud!' she said. 'That's for the pseuds who dance on the telly, y'know? I mean, the ones with the Saint Vitus tangos and that lot. Me, I like the good disco stuff and reggae—I *loved* Bob Marley—but with a band like this, you can't hear the beat. It's limp!'

I took her by a dangling elbow and led her back across the room.

'*Ç'est pas mon genre!*' I said.

'What's that mean? Is it French?'

'It is,' I said. 'It means I prefer the old-fashioned. It's more graceful.'

She looked at me with the hurt blue eyes of a baby, nothing to compare with Fidelia's, but beautiful in their own right. I picked my way through the boxing slitherers and coat-hangers, and went to the bar for a goblet of champagne, but I had far better at home. I suspected a dash of cider.

A disastrous night. I left that awful noise and the shuffle of feet, found the car and drove off, so thankfully, to a bit of peace and a decent drink.

But I was thinking of Fidelia.

34

THE DAYS following I can only describe as demonic. The papers came on us as a flood. The situation in Iran and the resultant break in oil supplies was our first interest, but our agents were alive to the threat of war with Iraq, and to the suffering of our labour force. Our agent in Khorramshahr radioed that we could have no idea of the way women and children were being forced into the dust. They were starving, they were thirsty, and there was nothing around them but privation. How could a baby survive? How could a mother save her sanity and her swollen-bellied child when there was no water? How could nurses do their duty? The doctors had gone, but for a few, and the few were students without sufficient knowledge. I gave instructions, but what did that mean? Exactly nothing.

I had no reach. No ship could put in anywhere without serious risk. But the thought of women and children under fire was an abomination. I thanked heaven that the Emir had installed an up-to-date telephone system and called Abol Hassan at the Um'm Sham'ms bazaar. I asked him to send a fleet of dhows up the coast to any available port where the people could board and get away, sail down to Kuwait, and reach the airport to be flown out to Alexandria.

The prolixity of that job could have turned a lot of our people into nut cases. Few of the refugees had any papers, though some had passports but without visas. My friends in Kuwait helped, the Egyptian consular staff was efficiency itself, and in a couple of weeks we had them all in Alexandria. We rented three floors of an hotel and they were happy, without any wish to leave. I agreed, because bringing them to London would have been enormously more expensive. Any expense went on my account with Iran, and I could sue for it, though knowing the Iranians I was sure I would be paid. They might have little interest in obeying international law, but in financial matters they remained strictly Islamic, upright and honest.

The bill for the dhows was pathetically small, considering what the crews had done, so I tripled it and gave the same amount to Abol Hassan.

I knew I had a friend there, and I kept the thought in mind that I might need him. In those matters, instinct is always right.

Meantime, pressure was building for the flower show. There seemed not very much to be done, when in reality there was a great deal, especially in the detail. I was amazed at the time and the care it took only to plant the exhibits, rack them, and store them in the refrigerator trucks.

Oil and flowers. A curious combination, though I was in the middle of it and I was amused by the thought. I had an appointment down at Greenhithe to welcome my first new tanker, and Captain Strömborg had invited me to luncheon. The helicopter came in and we flew through glorious weather over some of the loveliest land in the world, and landed alongside the ship. She was dressed overall in signal flags and bunting, with the captain waiting to escort me up the gangway to be piped aboard by the bo'suns.

I got a first good heave of my favourite smell of crude, and I was almost back at Um'm Sham'ms where that whiff came in when the wind fell. I was almost home, back on that quiet shore.

We went over the ship's papers, all highly satisfactory, and then to the dining room. Over a very good luncheon cooked by a Chinese chef, Captain Strömborg told me the ship's news and said that the men knew of the seamen's strike and advised that a ten percent rise was in order so that he could sail on time.

'Give them twenty percent,' I said. 'You'll have a happy ship.'

'Isn't it too much? They've got quarters like an hotel, they eat the best, plenty of time off, and I think ten percent is enough!'

'You're the master. Ten percent it shall be!'

I got back to the helicopter absolutely content and flew back by a different route, another superb landscape, with more forest and plenty of ploughland, and I was surprised how far from any built-up area we were at The Cherish. I was glad those Portkabins were in place.

But the house echoed. There was, in fact, nobody there. Mrs Hubbleston had left a cold buffet for me, tomato soup on the spirit burner, sliced lamb, a salad of peeled, finely-chopped tomatoes and onions, a cheese tray, and a bowl of fruit, but the light still held and I had no wish to eat.

The emptiness of the house troubled me, but why I shall never be able to tell. All my life I had been alone, though there were always dozens of people nearby to talk to, and perhaps that had given me the feeling of being able to subsist without companionship.

Certainly, standing there looking out of the window, I knew it to be untrue.

I felt alone, neglected, even bereaved.

And afraid.

It took sheer mental and even physical struggle to turn from the window and look at the gloom between me and the French windows in the library. Ridiculous, but it seemed crowded with the ghosts of people whose home it had been through the generatons. I made a sudden turn and reached the lights and switched them all on. Better. But still that lonely feeling gnawed. I could have filled the place with people, but I had chosen not to. There was

plenty of room for seven secretaries, but it was a base
thought and outlandish. A man, afraid of the dark. Of
an empty house?

What type of man?

The telephone's ring sent a ripple up my spine and yet
induced a happy feeling that I was not forgotten, that I
had at least contact with my world.

'Hullo?'

'Jon? I'm in the neighbourhood. May I slip in for a
drink?'

'Stay for a cold supper, by all means!'

'Ah, marvellous. My train's not till ten-thirty and
everything round here's shut. So I get to London, no
restaurant car, and London's dead at two in the morning.
Be there in ten minutes!'

I breathed in a long, uneven lungfill and I was myself
again, though painfully aware of a weak spot that
possibly I would never root out. A debilitating thought.

Hilsly came in almost as a typhoon, slung his fur coat
on a chair, tried to throw his hat over a lamp and missed,
and poured himself a drink.

'Thank God I'm back to civilisation!' he said, lifting
the glass. 'This and my friend over there are the only
things keeping me alive. I can't stop feeling cold. It *can't*
be what they call spring! Did you have the same trouble
when you first came back?'

'Can't say I did.'

'I've been up to the new factory. Going up a treat in
spite of the cold. I don't know why it's said that the
British workman's no good. They're damn near finished.
But I had to stay at one of those hotels, y'know, where
the bar shuts at tea-time and you can't buy a bottle of
whisky even by prayer. I went over the machinery today.
It's all there. We'll be working in a month. We've stolen
a march on everybody. We've got a three-year order
book. It's millions. And we've only just started!'

187

'Sounds good.'

'It's simply tremendous, that's what. I need another million!'

'I've seen no correspondence?'

'What for?'

'Is a million so little?'

'In what *we're* doing, yes. In any event you can well afford it, can't you?'

'I'll have to look at the figures first. There *are* other shareholders?'

'Of course. But I wanted to keep it among ourselves. You see that, don't you?'

'Very clearly. It's illegal. You were too long in Iran, where anything went. Try that sort of thing here, and you have to face corporation and company law. And our judges are extremely strict!'

Hilsly was sitting forward, elbows on knees, with the crystal between his hands. His knuckles showed white. He looked at me underbrow.

'I remember once BB's saying you'd never make a good businessman,' he said. 'Now I know what he meant.'

'I remember the incident, too. Some of you tried to cheat the Omanis out of a considerable sum of money and three of their ships. I refused to sign. One doesn't risk years in prison for the sake of money. Haven't you learned that? Obviously, one of BB's little ironies.'

He stood, downed the rest of his drink, and put his glass on the sideboard.

'I came here for dinner, not a lecture! Second thoughts, I won't stay for dinner. I'm disappointed. I thought I had a friend!'

'You have a very good friend. But he's a careful one. My auditors will be at your office at nine in the morning. Let them have all they require.'

'Or else?'

'I'll put in a receiver. I'll foreclose!'

He went across to pick up his hat, came back and threw his coat over a shoulder, turned at the door to say something, thought better, and went out to the front door and closed it with an angry slam. I was alone again, but feeling better. Something was wrong. An apparently unplanned visit made into an airy request for a million pounds as if it were tenpence? Too obviously, something was wrong.

I called the London office and asked the operator to find Ed Hulles. He was on the line in a couple of minutes.

'I want you to go down to the Brent factory and give the books a thorough inspection,' I said. 'Don't permit yourself to be fobbed off. Say what you want and see that you get it. Any trouble, call me. Understood?'

'Perfectly, sir. I've had a feeling something was wrong there.'

'Why?'

'Odd little reports in the *Financial Times*. Credit-squeeze prattle. After all, we're the top of all the cash-flow companies. I saw no reason for it. Tewkes Industries is a very strong complex. The Brent side is particularly strong, according to reports. Something wrong, sir?'

'I want you to push a very cold muzzle into everything you find, and get on to me, here. All right? Good night.'

I had just lit the spirit stove to warm the soup when the doorbell rang. *Brrp-bp!* I might have dropped anything I was holding.

I went out to the hall and looked through the peeper.

Fidelia.

Beautiful as ever, in high colour from the cold wind, and smiling whitest teeth. A joy of joys at any time, but now more joyous still.

35

WHILE I served the lamb I was regaled with an almost minute-by-minute saga of our arrival at Chelsea and the more-than-six-hour transference of greenstuff from the trucks to the cold rooms, and the staff's dependence on the tea and coffee and sandwiches they had taken with them.

'Why not take a catering van?' I asked her. 'You'd at least have hot meals at the proper time?'

'No place to park it. They're very strict. We'll have to go to *their* places. Won't be as good or anything near, but there'll be no troub'. Besides, it's only for a week, isn't it? When are you going to join us?'

'Perhaps on the second or third day.'

'And miss the awards?'

'I have to meet a tanker. If there *are* any awards, you take them. You worked for them!'

'Doesn't seem fair. You put a lot of money into it, you know. You ought to be there!'

'Money's nothing. It's knowledge and capability, that's what counts!'

'All three together's what matters. Without them, nothing, and without your help I couldn't have moved. *Do* try to be there.'

Chewing the lamb and a redcurrant jelly piquance, I imagined how it would be if this sort of meal, this sort of talk could go on through the years, and I found it pleasant to think about.

'Do *try* to be there,' she said again, her hand in mine at the door. 'I've enjoyed tonight so much!'

'I'm delighted you came. It saved a lonely dinner. And your taxi's honking!'

She leaned forward and kissed me, the merest zephyr.

'Good night!' she called from the lane. 'See you when!'

I went to bed on a pink and pale-blue cloud.

But it came off in the morning with a call from Miss Moriarty to report that Hilsly was in St Breda's hospital in critical condition, and asking for me. That turned my day around.

He was full of tubes and on some sort of machine when I got there, and unable to talk. He looked awful.

'Cirrhosis,' a doctor said, over my shoulder. 'And alcoholic hepatitis. Couple of bottles of whisky a day don't improve matters, do they?'

'Any hope?'

'Possibly not. Or not for very long. He's a long-term case of self-indulgence.'

'You'll do your best?'

'Of course. But what's to prevent him boozing his way out once we've put him on his feet?'

But I had a feeling. Why was Hilsly back on the bottle? Something was wrong in the business. An extra million was needed. Why?

Miss Moriarty gave me most of the reasons when she came in on the following morning.

'Gambling debts,' she said, opening a large file. 'He was among too many sheikhs. They don't care about money. It's our invention, not theirs. They use what they've got. Mister Hilsly tried to keep up with them. He used what he had. It wasn't enough. He has five court cases against him. A total of more than two million pounds.'

'Consult the lawyers. Pay the total. Warn all the clubs that I'll sue if he's ever allowed to play again. Pay him a nominal salary to his home address once a month. Take him off the Board of Directors. Now, who's the smartest man we've got?'

'Mister Gault, I'd say.'

191

'A letter, please. Addressed to Mister Hilsly at Saint Breda's. *When your physicians have assured me that you are fit again, we shall meet to discuss your future. Your gambling debts are paid. Your salary continues. Get really well soon. Yours ever.* And please get me Mister Gault on the phone.'

Mister Gault really did have something on his chest. I heard almost in disbelief a catalogue of damning complaints that I cut off in mid-spate to tell him to come to the office immediately and bring the files with him.

Miss Moriarty's choice told of the ability to spot a winner. Alexander Gault, in his early thirties and speaking with a ring of the Doric, was a man of many good parts, not least a diamond-edge way with words.

'I'm glad to have this opportunity,' he said, after an opening ten minutes of unrestrained attack on poor Hilsly. 'I'd have resigned this week and come to see you. It's as bad as that!'

'Give me the areas where the trouble is.'

'Three. Sales. Engineering programs. And new models. We need them. We've got a fine work force. None better in the world. But they're being misused.'

'How?'

'They're constructing two-year-old models. We've got a much finer product. They all know it, and they wonder.'

'But Hilsly told me you have a three-year order book. What happened?'

'We had. We haven't now. First, production. Then, sales. Then, outlets. Here, the United States and Canada, and Europe, to mention the biggest. We've nothing to fear from Japan or Hong Kong or Taiwan, for a change. Even if they copied us, it'd take them three years to come on the market. We could be there now!'

I made a decision.

'Go back to your office as managing director. Issue

192

your orders with a copy to me. If you need money, let me know. I think that should be all?'

'I wish everything were as clear-cut!' he said.

'Where are the grey patches?'

'His pals on the board. His sales staff. Hangers-on. Leeches. Toadies!'

'Sack the lot!'

'I wish we'd had this talk long before. Still, one or two weeks with the rotten wood chopped off, and we'll be shipshape. I'll guarantee that. Will I have control over sales?'

'You're managing director, aren't you?'

'Very well, sir. I've got somebody first-class to take charge of the United States and Canada. She's an American and top of the tree, and she'll shake them up, at long last!'

'Good. You're in favour of women in top positions?'

He stood, smiling.

'A woman with a brain is the finest salesman of the lot. She's had to compete twice as hard as the men. I believe you'll see a difference. I'll send her this week. No objections?'

'None.'

'Good. I'm off. I'm grateful for this. Hilsly and his bottle of whisky on the desk and all those barnacles helping him ruin the company were a lot too much. I've been in electronics since I was eleven. It's always been in my blood. I feel I've got the finest job in the world. Will I be having the same salary as Hilsly?'

'I'm glad you retain a Scottish sense of values. Of course. I shall make that clear in my letter to you confirming your position as managing director with complete control over all departments. Is that satisfactory?'

'Perfectly, sir. M'wife's in hospital waiting our baby. May I go?'

I had a good mind to go down to the factory then and

there, but I felt I should give Gault a chance to settle things, and then go. I asked Miss Moriarty to send hand-delivered letters to all the board members that because of company reconstruction, their services would no longer be needed but their fees would be paid to the end of the year.

I had expected something of a storm, but I was amazed by the combined attack of twenty-four board members and their legal staffs. At The Cherish there were twenty-eight Telexes, telegrams, notes of telephone calls, and more coming in. I ignored them and went to bed. I think there is nothing so good as getting into warmth in warmed pyjamas and sending the world to hell, and especially the fatheads expecting me to reverse my decision to sack them. I have never had anything but contempt for drunks, particularly those interfering in business, and to find part of my business being ruined by alcoholics made me angry. I had no sympathy for any of them. Hilsly, of course, I had to treat a little differently. He had been a colleague for many years and had fast ties to BB and Frukey. I *had* to treat him differently, though I had no intention of allowing him back into the company.

The death of his wife, the horror of Iran, the burning of his house, were all matters for sympathy. I intended he should live easily for the rest of his life, and that was that.

36

FERGUSON, MY chief of security, stopped the car at the gate, and I pressed the window button for him to put his head in.

'We got a report from the police, sir,' he said. 'There

were three blokes in the village last night. Dark jobs. They came down here and circled the place. The police went after them and took them to the station. All students. All over thirty and students? So they were told to shove off and not come nigh again. The car was hired. It's being looked into. I think you should have another man in the car, sir. He'll shoot first and form'late his questions after. If that suits you, sir?'

'It does, and thank you. I shan't be back tonight.'

'All be safe enough, sir.'

It was costing me over six thousand pounds a month for the men and the dogs, fine Alsatians, specially trained to track down and attack any stranger. I gave little for their chances. Even so, it seemed ridiculous to pay that sort of bill annually for a thin sheath of security. But I know Arabs, or I think I do, and once they have taken an oath, it stays in molten metal until what was sworn is accomplished.

Time was always a brother to them.

My newest tanker, sister-ship of six, was moored at Greenwich in spanking new paint and bright brass, and I was piped aboard what I had almost designed for myself. Midships I had a suite in teak and mahogany, carpeted with the best from the Iranian market, with two bathrooms of equal luxury from Germany, a kitchen styled in Paris, and a real supermarket in miniature from Pec of Milan—in short, a fairy tale come true and real only for me.

And my wife.

Who?

I'd thought about the entire business for too long without any real conclusion. I realised I was a creature of settled habit. If I wanted to get up in the small hours to write notes or read reports, I did, but I knew I might disturb a partner unless we had separate rooms, an unattractive prospect.

Miss Moriarty? An extremely pleasant girl, quite beautiful and a real brain, Master of Arts, Oxon. Miss Marriott? A chartered accountant with an off-beat sense of humour that occasionally lightened the more humdrum office hours, and not least, the choice of Mrs Pincus as her replacement, no small honour. But as women to marry?

No.

It would have been like bringing the office back home with me.

Of all the princesses, honourables, and other lovely women I had met socially, many of whom had tried to grab me, no, too. I made little of my social life. I attended luncheons and dinners and private parties in London, Paris, and where-not, but still no. I took one of them home, but when she took her wig off and cleansed the cosmetics, I found her far less a woman than any of those who'd made me a gift of themselves, either on the bed in Um'm Sham'ms or on the office carpet. In fact, I felt far more love in memory of all of them than I felt for anyone I'd met since.

Except, of course, Fidelia.

She had amazed and confounded me by the change in her appearance at the Hunt Ball. But if that was a reason for marrying, it escaped me. To marry was to join a life. I was not sure that she was drawn to me. I had made no effort to get nearer to her. All our meetings out in the greenhouses or the garden or in the office were pleasantly impersonal, though they left me with a fine sense of her fragrance, her *self*.

I was even unsure if she had anybody on a string, although it had occurred to me more than once that such a girl must have a trail of handsome lads.

That's what I was not.

Or anything near it.

I was a sunburned crisp, with a great deal of money, true.

196

But as a life-partner?

Nothing much.

All rather puzzling, but then, I had other matters to think about, and the non-war brewing between Iran and Iraq was far from the smallest. It had not yet affected our oil supplies to any great extent, and any gaps could be filled in from other fields. My worry was the old hatred between the two countries and their allies, and I foresaw vast destruction to industry, not to mention the human side of it—the deaths, the suffering and the abiding grief. How it was to be assuaged was far beyond the realm of man. I realised, so drearily, that I could do nothing, and the few I managed to help would be under hourly threat of assassination wherever they happened to be.

And so was I.

Not an encouraging thought, and the security man beside the driver was a reminder that even in my own country I was anything but safe. Would a wife be safer?

I looked over my hotel ship next, just out of her berth, and found her a beautiful example of our workmanship. She had been a supertanker, but the designers had divided her space into single, double, and family cabins, with plenty of space for the children. The return fare between London and New York would be about a hundred pounds, all in, with self-service buffets almost at cost catering, and a first-class staff internationally recruited to ensure that no language problems would crop up. I imagined the happiness of a couple walking down those corridors to their family cabin and opening the door to carpeting, warm colours and comfortable beds, and then to the cafeteria with a varied menu of excellent food at half the price elsewhere, supervised playrooms and workshops for the children, and then a bar without the burden of duty or tax.

This was my primary target, tax of any kind.

Tax of any kind should not exist.

Income tax was an idiocy introduced for the prosecution of the Napoleonic wars, and later, when idiocy went into remission, temporarily repealed.

The idiots were still in charge.

37

IT WAS a late bluish evening when Fidelia's father called again, and I invited him in for a drink. He was fairly tall and white-haired and, to my mind, a thoroughly nice man. He had the rosy cheeks of country life, and he gave off a scent of tweed, nothing to his disadvantage.

We went to the drinks tray, and he poured himself a dram with a dash from the siphon, and sat on the arm of the sofa—a man used to emergency calls?—while I poured a small dose without soda, and joined him.

'Lovely!' he said. 'Your very good health. I needed this. A birth at four this morning. Surgery at nine, and a round of calls till now. Glad to say, nothing very much wrong. Healthy lot, by and large. One of the church masons broke two fingers in a granite-slab fall. Plaster bandage and some sleeping pills, off like a fly. They're doing a fine job at the church. It'll be the pride of the place, thanks to you!'

'It wasn't supposed to be known!'

'Oh, it isn't. Don't worry. But some of us can add two and two!'

'Thanks from a man of your standing is thanks enough. If anything more's needed, I hope you'll let me know. It's little enough for the sort of life I lead here. Never been happier!'

'Mm. Delighted. The other thing I came here for. I'm still concerned about danger to Fidelia.'

'Danger?'

'Well, there *are* those sentry boxes, and a team of burlies and dogs that're fairly new?'

'I'm the target, as I said. Certainly not those I employ. Fidelia? No danger at all. If I thought there was the merest sniff, I'd send them all home. That brings up another matter, Doctor Leigh.'

'What's that?'

'Would you have any objection to my asking Fidelia to marry me?'

I waved to the tray, and he got up and went for a refill shorter than the first.

'I'm going to point out that Fidelia is long beyond my jurisdiction,' he said, his back to me. 'She'd want our approval, of course. She's that sort of girl. But in anything she wants, we've never been able to stop her. You'll have to ask her!'

'I shall do so tomorrow at the show.'

He turned to me and raised his glass.

'Pretty abrupt sort of fellow, aren't you?' he said, laughing.

'How often are you, or can you afford to be, hesitant with your patients?'

'Touché. I agree. May I ask? Where would you live?'

'Here, primarily. But several times a year I have to go to New York and other places on business. She'd always come with me. Any objection?'

'None whatever. She's always loved to travel. She loves the French cathedrals. And Venice and Florence. Did a backpack tour when she got her degree. About travel you'll never have the smallest worry. Any excuse to get out of the village, and she's off!'

The telephone rang.

'Probably for me,' he said. 'I've got a bad case at the hospital. I told them where I was going. May I?'

I nodded and he lifted the receiver. I walked out to

the downstairs cloakroom and used those moments to rid myself of a burden. I went back far happier.

'That was Fidelia,' he said, in a wide smile. 'You've taken seven awards, top of the show. You may have three more coming. Her delight was that her favourite orchids took the gold. Roses as well. I gather it must've been the devil of a day down there. She wanted to know why you weren't there?'

'Other things to do. But I'll be there tomorrow. Wish I'd been there today, dammit. But I've got ships and whatnot to look after. I'm so glad for her. She's worked so hard!'

'That's how she—'

An ambulance-clang drowned us.

'Jesus!' he said. 'That's for me. Thanks for the drink. This is for a girl I hope I'm *not* going to lose. I'm afraid I may. Not the ideal thought to go to bed with. So often I'm sickened.'

'You have the worst job,' I said, and tapped his back as we walked to the door. 'We often forget it. But God love you *every* moment!'

He turned sharp on the steps and speared me with those grey eyes.

'Are you a godly man?' he asked, quietly.

'I'd never say so. I'd say I'm a believer in the Western and the Muslim faiths. I believe there *is* an almighty spirit, but I don't argue about it. I simply have faith!'

'That's all any of us have. Come up to the house for dinner. The best roast beef and Yorkshire pudding in the country. My wife's contribution to international cuisine. Fidelia will arrange it. Good night!'

I saw him go, and the ambulance turned to follow, and the security men opened the gate. Some of us are born to alleviate, to console, and to prevent disease and pain. He was one, and I hoped for his patient.

Radio Four was on, and I listened to the news from

Ireland and the Basque country, nothing from the Middle East, an item about pandas from China, but nothing real about the calamity of economic recession throughout the world. Some talked about economics without the faintest idea of what they were talking about, or involvement. They had *no* idea, whether in energy, transport, banking or industry—pretty well the four sides of our problem—with, of course, greed in the middle.

A little time before nine I had a call from Fidelia, but on a bad line of crackle and buzz, and she told me of the awards. I said I would be down next day for luncheon and I wanted them all round the table. She could barely hear me or I her, but I swore I would put in a new telephone system on the radio grid and finish the plug-in-and-bawl blither for aye. I could talk to my Arabian friends as if they were in the same room, but not to people in my own country?

Rubbish.

I was in too much of a temper to read, and I went to bed in what Frukey called a pet, which makes you kick even shoes out of the way.

As if it were their fault.

Poor subservient nothings.

We're a funny lot.

Pretending so much, and kicking shoes.

38

I SUPPOSE the most glorious shock of my life was the sight of our part of the flower show.

Fidelia had designed a marvellous display. I had seen

only the sketches and the growing plants, but it took imagination to see the end result. I saw it then, but not before, and I was floored.

I had never known that the colour and the scent of flowers could exact such a wonderful penalty. I was stopped in the doorway by sight and smell. The only time I had known anything like it was in the Emir's garden and Frukey's smaller copy at Um'm Sham'ms, looked after by the Emir's gardeners. In the evening, positively a place of delight, with icy beer, goatflesh kebabs, and French pastry tartlets. How many evenings I whiled away there without knowing how lucky I was.

But I knew then, and I thought my thanks to the Emir for those years of pleasure, and now to Fidelia for her insistence on what she wanted. She had been right. Events proved what she had imagined. That, too, is a wonder of our lives. How is it that the imaginations of some of us are able with a little help to create a joyous world they have never seen? Or that we may only imagine and never see? That, I think, is the original human problem. We are all able to imagine, but most of us for some reason cannot bring it into being.

I wondered in that marvel of colour—in which I could see the genius of Fidelia and her lovely friends—why in the name of God, if we could bring this beauty into our lives with some carpentry and the eager strength of bulb and shrub planting, it could not be done in other ways and in other areas, even reaching to Government and the sad incidence of national policy.

Fidelia came toward me, and I kissed both her hands.

'You've done something absolutely wonderful!' I said. 'From what you showed me on paper and all those plants, I could never have imagined this. It's amazing!'

'Worth the effort? And the cost?'

'What's cost beside this?'

She laughed, a whisper in the rumble of the crowd

round about, and turned, hand in mine, and led to the left. I loved the feel of that hand, so assuring.

We strolled along the crowded, scented lanes and looked at masses of violets, snowdrops, crocuses, so many colours, all of them held back in the cold rooms by the florist's art, and then to the roses, a love of glorious blossom, from the dwarf varieties in front to the tall girls in the rear and then the ramblers at the back. I never knew their names, especially the Latin, and never cared about learning. It was enough that I saw and identified and knew the names I was used to. A hell of a gardener, but I never pretended I was more than a clerk enmeshed in the oil business, because that is what I was. The rest was merest whim, and it pleased me.

We found a tea-time corner, and I ordered a pot of coffee and a plate of éclairs, my favourite pastry.

'Come home,' Fidelia said. 'Mummy makes the best éclair of the lot. She learned from the chef at the Plaza-Athénée. They were staying there before I was born. I believe it was their honeymoon hotel. I think it's the best hotel in the world. I only ever spent a night there. I love the Relais. A little plate there, and a salad, and you can face the day!'

'You like Paris?'

'So much. It's a darling place. You can do as you like. You can do that in London or New York or anywhere else if you think so. But it's not the same. Paris is completely different. It's so beautifully French!'

'How long have you had this feeling for Paris?'

'Since I went there the first time. My first love was a Frenchman. He was killed in Chad. Such a lovely man. Sweet. I can still feel his tongue. I whirl on it. And what? Nothing!'

'You mean that some Gascon with a titillating tongue is more important than anyone else?'

'So far!'

'Well, supposing someone else had a tongue?'

'Something to think about!'

The waitress came with the coffee and the éclairs, and in her shuffle of putting them down, I looked at Fidelia. She seemed lost inside herself with that smiling glaze of eye that tells of pleasure.

The thought that she had ever been to bed with someone had never burdened my mind, but burden is what it most certainly was proving to be. I could never have believed it had she not told me, clear and direct. More, I respected her honesty. Not every girl would pull aside the curtains like that. Some memories are better forgotten, I suppose, though I could think of none in my life, surely none that were intimate. It's odd what goes through people's heads.

'Still thinking of your Frenchman?' I asked.

She blinked in a stare, and laughed, awake.

'No! I missed an award for our roses. It won't happen again. I was thinking of that hummock beyond the garden, and if we could bulldoze it to a shallower slope for perfect drainage. Then set stones in a design, brick the paths, and dig in about ten tons of farmyard manure with a few bags of Chilean nitrate, and let it lie fallow for the winter. I'd like six more girls and ten more men for the dig?'

'You choose them. And buy the hummock, before you start. Who's it belong to? Sam Bellows?'

'That's him. I'll get it for a song. His sheep were always a nuisance. We'll be rid of *them*, for openers!'

'You'll have quite a staff there, won't you?'

'Wait till you see our orders. We're really in business. We ought to show a good fat profit!'

'We're in it only for profit?'

'Everything's got to show a profit, hasn't it? No use having a place like ours and no profit. I think you'll be pleased with this year's. Over seventy percent!'

'Seventy? Sounds like good business. I had no idea!'

'It's better than most. I'd like to go in for vegetables. There's a big market for them. I don't mean your ordinary cabbages and carrots, either. Endive, red lettuce, mange-touts, enormous asparagus. Lots of things.'

'Sounds as though you'll need more land?'

'There's enough for the buying.'

'Buy it.'

She put her hands together.

'Lovely!' she said. 'Wait till next year. You won't know us!'

'I'll take a bet on that!'

The waitress gave me the bill, and I put a couple of notes in her hand.

'You can come again!' she said, looking at them. 'Ol' Santa Claus don't come this often. Enjoy your coffee, then, sir?'

'Did indeed. Save that table for tomorrow afternoon, same time, will you?'

'That'll get done, sir,' she said, whipping the napkin at crumbs and winking broadly at Fidelia. 'No doubt about *that*!'

I went across to the cashier and gave her the bill. While I reached for the money I sensed rather than felt a presence of threat. I ducked to the left, and was seared by the hot flash of a bullet that hit the wall in front. I knew that bullet would have carved deeper into me than the wall. As the cashier screamed, I kept down and turned in time to see Fidelia's long blue arm pick up an orchid in a silver-papered pot and throw. From his pelt, he was an Arab. The pot hit square across the bridge of his nose and knocked him down, bursting in shards that left blood running. Fidelia's boot finished him with a kick to the temple.

'Watch it, sir!' a security guard bellowed, letting a dog

205

off the leash and following in a run to my right. There were so many people all shouting that I saw nothing until a man came through, obviously from the Gulf, and aimed a gun at me. But the dog had him by the cuff and the shot went over my head and into the glass roof, and splinters showered, tinkling, and the screams grew louder. Police were pushing the crowd into small groups and going through them in a far-from-pleasant search, looking, I supposed, for more guns.

A detective-sergeant walked with me back to the tabel.

'We'll need statements from you and the young lady, sir,' he said, hovering over us as I sat and took Fidelia's hands in mine.

'In a few moments, Sergeant. All right?'

He crossed the room again, his back as expressionless as his wide face.

'You saved my life,' I said to Fidelia. 'Sounds banal enough, doesn't it?'

'I don't know about banal,' she said, trying to smile. 'I certainly saved my job!'

'You guaranteed it for life. Delia, I've got plenty to think about. Oil, shipping, hovercraft, computers, construction, the Channel Tunnel—a dozen different areas—and behind it there's always the threat that someone's going to bob up with a gun. It's on the cards I'm a goner. I don't expect it to lessen. In fact, after today, I think it'll get worse. They'll keep trying.'

'But what *for*?'

'It's a curse and a pledge. I became mixed up in a family—what?—well, a sort of quarrel. The worst sort. One or another swore to kill me. So far, I've come through. This fracas was first blood. I'm afraid it won't be the last. Having all that in mind, will you marry me?'

She looked at me, upper lip under bottom teeth, and her hands tightened.

206

'If I thought you meant that?' she said, barely heard through the noise still going on.

'I *mean* it. Will you?'

'*Yes*. On one condition?'

That stopped me cold.

'Well?'

'That we honeymoon at the Plaza-Athénée!'

I took her and kissed her full on a bruised-rose mouth.

'On!' I said—how much later?—finding a breath. 'I love you, in case you were wondering?'

'I wasn't!'

Imagine?

Nice?

Lovely!

I seemed to stand again on the quiet shore of Um'm Sham'ms, remembering Frukey and BB, and all the girls, and Khalil and his father, and Abd and Hamid.

I wanted to keep alive that moment of beauty and, more, the spirit summed for me in Fidelia's love.

I wanted to relax, to warm myself, to grow in its heat.

I wanted our children to be nurtured in it.

In the radiant love of a woman, might we not all learn from Isaiah to receive 'beauty for ashes, the oil of joy for mourning, the garment of praise for the spirit of heaviness'?

A good, open-ended question, one worth answering and glowing with all hope.

Fidelia's father proposed it in his toast to us after a wedding breakfast on the village green.

I have cherished it ever since.

Vivat! One of my few words of Latin, and the best.

NEL BESTSELLERS

ORBIT	*Thomas Block*	£1.95
FOREFATHERS	*Nancy Cato*	£2.50
THE CITADEL	*A. J. Cronin*	£1.95
SCHISM	*Bill Granger*	£1.75
MAURA'S DREAM	*Joel Gross*	£2.25
FRIDAY	*Robert Heinlein*	£2.50
THE WHITE PLAGUE	*Frank Herbert*	£2.50
SHRINE	*James Herbert*	£2.25
CHRISTINE	*Stephen King*	£2.50
SPELLBINDER	*Harold Robbins*	£2.50
THE CASE OF LUCY B.	*Lawrence Sanders*	£2.50
ACCEPTABLE LOSSES	*Irwin Shaw*	£1.95

All these books are available at your local bookshop or newsagent, or can be ordered direct from the publisher. Just tick the titles you want and fill in the form below.

NEL P.O. BOX 11, FALMOUTH TR10 9EN, CORNWALL

Postage Charge:

U.K. Customers 45p for the first book plus 20p for the second book and 14p for each additional book ordered to a maximum charge of £1.63.

B.F.P.O. & EIRE Customers 45p for the first book plus 20p for the second book and 14p for the next 7 books; thereafter 8p per book.

Overseas Customers 75p for the first book and 21p per copy for each additional book.

Please send cheque or postal order (no currency).

Name ....

Address ....

....

Title...

While every effort is made to keep prices steady, it is sometimes necessary to increase prices at short notice. New English Library reserve the right to show on covers and charge new retail prices which may differ from those advertised in the text or elsewhere. (A)